Murder Paints a Portrait

By the same author
Polmarron Tower
The Bride of Invercoe
The Wolves of Monte Neve
The Spirit and the Heritage
Rowdy Rhymes and Rec-im-itations
A View from the Dart
Vulgar Verse and Variations
Dublin Year Book

MURDER PAINTS A PORTRAIT

Vincent Caprani

GLENDALE

First published in Ireland
by Glendale Publishing Ltd.
4 Haddington Terrace
Dunlaoghaire
Co. Dublin

© 1992 Vincent Caprani

All rights reserved. No part of this publication may be
reproduced, stored in a retrieval system, or transmitted, in
any form or by any means, electronic, mechanical,
photocopying, recording or otherwise, without the prior
permission of the publisher.

British Library Cataloguing in Publication Data

A catalogue record of this book is available
from the British Library

ISBN 0 907606 98 9

Origination by Wendy A. Commins, The Curragh
Printed in Ireland by Colour Books Ltd., Dublin

1

The blonde was the most photogenic piece of scenery around. Goddard thought hard about getting a few quick shots of her as she stepped down into the boat. She moved well, gracefully, like a dancer or perhaps a fashion model, and then stood for a few moments with her legs spread out, bracing herself against the pitch and the roll of the boat. The sea breeze whipped the fawn-coloured trenchcoat about her, moulding the light fabric to the shape of her long legs.

Goddard got in a few quick shots of the mainland harbour, the fishing boats, the spray and the white waves curling and breaking along the rocky shoreline and as he was on the point of swinging the camera round and trying one or two sneak shots of the blonde she suddenly sat down, turning her back to him. Later maybe.

He snapped the leather flap over the camera snout and sat down also, edging a bit further along the starboard seat so that he was only an arm's length from her. Her face was in profile now. The golden-blonde hair was scraped back severely and simply from a finely shaped face. Her eyes were large and solemn and grey-flecked. Goddard, not wanting to be caught staring, glanced about at the other occupants of the motor-launch, which was now *put-put-putting* and rocking gently as it moved away from the jetty.

The boatman was a small, weather-tanned old-timer in yellow oilskins and a greasy mariner's cap. The only other passenger that morning besides the blonde and Goddard was a big giant of a man in his late fifties. He had close-cropped iron-grey hair, granite jaw, scar on cheek, and a dented and flattened nose which suggested he may have been a boxer at one time. He sat forward, with his elbows on his knees, all the while tapping the knurled fist of one ham-like hand into the open palm of the other and staring down silently at the little runs of bilge water lapping against his boots.

'Cigarette?'

The big fellow looked up slowly, not really noticing at first the cigarette packet which Goddard was pushing towards him; then, when the invitation gradually cut through his thoughts, he shook his head politely and from his pocket drew out a pipe and a tobacco tin. He filled the pipe absently, fingering black tobacco into it without looking at it, or Goddard, or at anything save the bilge water. He put the pipe in his mouth, but didn't light it.

'Cigarette?'

Goddard was much more interested in the blonde's response. But she was a bigger disappointment. She didn't even look at him, just shook her head and continued staring out at the soapy crests of the waves with those big beautiful grey-flecked eyes. A real jolly crew, Goddard frowned, cupping his hands around a cigarette and a fourth guttering match before swaying up to the man at the wheel.

'Cigarette?'

'That's right decent of you sir,' the old-timer grinned, plucking two from the packet and putting them somewhere inside his oilskin jacket.

'How long will it be?'

'Another twenty minutes will see us snug and sound.'

But the journey seemed endless. The route to the island was exposed, catching the full force of the Atlantic swell between the mainland and the island. The motor launch went racing up on the crest of each wave with unchanging regularity. Every once in a while a big freakish wave would lift the boat up above the other waves, holding it tremulously for a fraction of a second, and then plunging it down into the next little sea valley as the wave fell away from the keel. Coming up on the distant horizon, way out behind the island, were some big black rain clouds. The boatman nodded towards them.

'She'll be gettin' up for a bit of a storm before the night's over. Wait'll you see.' The weathered, walnut face was crinkled with weather lore.

'What's it like, the island?'

'Quiet, this time of year. Most of the holiday folk is already gone by the end of September.'

'What do the local people do?'

'Count their takin's for the season, put up the shutters, hibernate for the winter, then come out next May and glitter up the place for another summer season.'

'And the hotel. What's it like?'

'Fine enough for these parts, but I imagine it's only fair to middlin' against them big places in Dublin or London. Would you be a London gent yourself, sir?'

'No, Dublin. I'm a freelance photographer.'

'That must be a nice class of work. Will you be stayin' long?'

'Depends. A day or two maybe.'

'Business or pleasure, if you don't mind me askin'?'

'Business,' Goddard replied, but when he glanced back once more to where the blonde was sitting he felt like adding 'and pleasure, if I'm lucky'.

Sometimes he was lucky. Not very often, but his line of work — travelling around quite a bit, occasionally photographing fashion models and starlets and publicity seekers — sometimes put him in the way of opportunities. Goddard rarely considered that his appearance might have something to do with it; he dressed well, was thirty years old, above average height, no beer belly — athletically built in fact – had dark hair and the kind of dark eyes that some women found appealing and romantic. And he carried himself with an easy self-assurance which owed nothing to a consciousness of how he looked.

'And will you be photographin' the scenery hereabouts?'

'Not really. Tell me, do you know most of the islanders?'

'Should do. I've been ferryman for upwards of thirty-five year.'

'Do you know a Mr Arthur Leon?'

There was a long pause — almost the beginning of an implacable silence — and then the boatman muttered: 'Him? He's not an islander.'

'He lives here, doesn't he?'

'Aye, but he's not what you'd call one of us.'

'But you know him?'

'I know him to see. That's all.'

'What can you tell me about him?'

There was another long pause, a kind of cautious hesitancy, in which the boatman seemed deeply engrossed in the task of carefully pointing the launch towards the narrow opening of the island's tiny harbour. Finally he muttered: 'People hereabouts have a sayin' — 'tis often that a man's mouth has broken his nose. Meanin' that if you can't speak good of someone then keep your silence.'

There was another brief pause followed by a quick change of tone. 'Here we are sir. Ten minutes ahead of skedoodle.'

The old-timer nosed the motor launch into the tiny harbour, cut off the engine, and let the boat glide up to the stone jetty. A man in a peaked cap and a black woollen gansey came down the steps, caught the line thrown to him from the launch and secured it through an iron ring affixed to the jetty wall just above the dark collar of seaweed. Then he knelt down to take the gunwale and steady the craft as the first passenger, the big man with the scar and the broken nose, quickly clambered out.

'Turnin' cool Jack. She's buildin' up for a pile of rain.'

But the big broken-nosed man said nothing and went quickly up the steps. Goddard turned to help the blonde with her travel bag. 'Allow me,' he smiled.

'I can manage.' She looked right through him.

Goddard shrugged, gathered up his own stuff, and then — with the launch still rocking gently back and forth and the boards slithery under his feet — climbed gingerly onto the stone platform. She was half way along the jetty before he caught up with her again.

'Are you staying at the hotel?'

She didn't answer.

'My name's Goddard. Joe Goddard. I'm a photographer and I'm —'

'Look,' she stopped suddenly, turning round to stare directly into his face. 'I've had blokes like you walk straight up to me before, blokes who try to walk in one side of your life and out the other. Know what I mean? Now just piss off sonny!'

And then she went up towards the hotel, walking smartly, the lithe easy sway of her neat little bottom like an angry rebuke. *Sonny*! Christ, she couldn't be more than 32 or 33 years of age! At the very most four or five years older than himself. And yet Goddard had to admit that there was an experienced, worldly, even hard-bitten, quality to her words that gave them a relevance.

She had a decided edge on him.

Goddard shrugged again. Win a few, lose a few. He paused at the end of the little pier, ostensibly to view his surroundings, in reality to avoid bumping into her so soon again at the hotel's reception desk. The main street — the only street in fact — rose steeply for a few hundred yards from the harbour and the hotel. It was flanked on either side by the usual buildings to be found in such places. First, directly opposite the hotel, was a boatyard and chandlery; then a row of solid two-storey houses, then a little stone church with a red-bricked National school adjoining it; a few more houses, a general store cum post office; then a chemist shop. Goddard crossed over the street when he saw the Kodak and Agfa signs. The chemist's window was chock full of dust-covered medicaments, veterinary appliances, cosmetics, polaroid glasses and tubes of sun tan lotion, the latter obviously intended for the summer visitors. There were no holiday makers to be seen. The door to the chemist shop was closed. The one, colourless street was almost totally deserted.

Goddard re-crossed the narrow street and entered the hotel. The blonde had already finished at the reception desk and a red-headed youth in a spotless white shirt and neat, tight-fitting black slacks was leading her upstairs and carrying her bags for her.

'Be with you in a moment sir,' the red-headed youth warbled down from the landing.

From the lobby Goddard had an excellent angle from which to catch another brief and tantalising view of her slim legs just before she disappeared from view. Then he carried his gear into the little cocktail bar directly across from the reception area, dumped the lot on an armchair and went to the bar. There was no one behind it, no one in sight. He rang the bell, waited a few minutes, rang it again, then dumped himself in one of the other armchairs and took in his surroundings.

The Hotel Bayview was like a lot of such places that he'd stayed in during the time he'd worked for the Tourist Board and the travel agents, out shooting scenic locations for their brochures and calendars. It was what Goddard categorised as an 'old colonels and dowagers retreat' — an elegant and sedate mid-Victorian house converted into an almost modern hotel; the old ceiling work and the ornate pilasters were retained along with a lot of gleaming wood panels, dark and heavy furniture, floral wallpaper, brasswork and mirrors and curlicued mahogany bits and pieces and a few heavily-gilt framed 'Monarch of the Glen' type prints. The place was 'lousy' with 'period' atmosphere. The only incongruities were the TV set, a cigarette vending machine, the gleaming beer pump handles and a few modernistic daubs of seascapes in aluminium frames.

'Dreadfully sorry for keeping you sir. I do apologise.' The red-haired youth came mincing into the cocktail bar with a flourish, a kind of visual and silent fanfare of trumpets. 'You did ring, didn't you?'

'Yes. I could do with a whiskey. Gold Label.'

'Certainly sir.' The youth waltzed in behind the narrow counter. 'We're rather short handed at the moment, I'm afraid. You see Mammy only takes on staff at the height of the season. She let the others go two weeks ago. Which makes yours truly a kind of maid of all work,' he giggled. The red tresses ran across his head from one ear to the other in corrugated ringlets, cascading down one side of his face in brilliant profusion and putting Goddard in mind of a concertina with the clasp broken. He had thin pointed features, neat and regular to the point of prettiness. 'There you are sir. Ice?'

'No thanks.' Goddard tipped some water from a counter

jug into the whiskey. 'You have a reservation in the name of Goddard?'

'Yes sir. And you must be Mr Goddard?'

'Uh-huh.' He raised the glass.

'Will you be staying long Mr Goddard?'

'It depends. Two or three days maybe. I've got to see a man named Leon. Arthur Leon. Do you know him?'

The youth turned his back, no longer face to face with Goddard. He was making a pretence of re-arranging some glasses on the shelf behind the bar.

'Well, do you know him?'

Without turning round the youth mumbled something about '... keeps to himself a lot ... never comes here anymore ....' then, quickly pirouetting out from behind the bar with a 'Oh, one moment sir ... I almost forgot ....' he minced back over to the reception desk and brought back the hotel register and a room key affixed to a plastic disc. 'Room 12, Mr Goddard. If you wouldn't mind signing the book now please.'

'Sure,' Goddard took the book and signed his name immediately under hers. Gloria Fontana, with an address in Kensington, London. *Gloria*? *Fontana*? It had to be a professional name. Chorus girl or fashion model? Or maybe a film starlet?

'Would you like me to take your luggage up now Mr Goddard?'

'No thanks. I can manage.' Goddard decided not to push the Leon enquiries. Not just yet anyway. He finished his drink quickly.

'Dinner is between eight and nine-thirty. Is that alright?'

'Fine.' He left a pound note tip on the counter.

'Ta indeed! Most generous Mr Goddard!'

Bloody extravagant, really. But Goddard was going to need some local information pretty soon. Besides, he knew he could put it down to expenses. He gathered up his pieces and went upstairs.

His room was clean, spacious and with a nice bay window view of the channel between the island and the mainland. He unpacked his things, hung them up, and later, in the shower, he went over the background to this present assignment. Goddard worked for a number of London magazines and newspapers in a freelance capacity, a kind of Irish 'man-on-the-spot' for any photo news — an IRA bombing, Papal visit, Irish Sweeps Derby, political summits, that sort of thing. Over the past few years the captions and comments tagged onto his photos had steadily grown into smallish news features and now he was more or less doubling as a photographer-journalist. The editor of one such magazine had phoned him five days ago and had commissioned him to get all he could on one, Arthur Leon. Who the hell was Arthur Leon, Goddard had asked. The London office had informed him that Leon was a product of London's 'Swinging Sixties' scene who had quickly made a name and some money for himself as a rather talented and innovative young artist. For a few years his canvasses, theatre sets, fabric designs and all that stuff had caught the mood of the times and had been all the rage. Then, almost as quickly, Arthur Leon had disappeared from the limelight and the gossip columns and vanished from the London scene. At the pinnacle of fame and success he had dropped from sight, his name soon relegated to the past and the limbo of yesterday's whizz kids. But a recent retrospective exhibition of his earlier work in a West End gallery had evoked and rekindled renewed interest in arty circles, creating curiosity about Leon's present whereabouts and his current work. Goddard's London editor had received a reliable tip-off that Leon was now living a kind of hermit-like existence on some remote island off the west coast of Ireland. And thus Goddard, as the man on the spot, was given the job of ferreting out the whereabouts and getting an interview. Simple — except that nobody so far wanted to talk about Leon, neither the ferryman or the hotel 'maid-of-all-work'. Why?

An hour later, freshly shaved and showered, in jeans and a clean grey polo neck sweater, the compact 35mm Nikon in the zipped-up pocket of his anorak, Goddard headed back down to the bar. The red-headed youth was in a white jacket this time, putting the finishing touches to a Gaelic coffee for a youngish, tweedish brunette with heavy-rimmed glasses who occupied the bay window seat. She had a couple of open books and a jotting pad spread out on the little table before her. The dark, scholarly glasses seemed to go with the hard-backed tomes. Intent on her books, her face was more than half-turned from Goddard's mildly inquisitive gaze. But her legs — she was absently scratching the left shin with the raised ankle of the right — were long and shapely. At least what he could see of them from below the hem of her tweed skirt. Goddard was still trying to gauge her face, and the full figure, as the youth danced back to the bar.

'Going out, Mr Goddard? Perhaps a teenie little drinkee prior to a perambulation, eh?'

'Yeah, only make it a big drinkee.'

'Pint?'

'Uh-huh. By the way ....' Goddard indicated the brunette with a brief, sidelong glance.

The earlier pound tip must have paid off because the maid-of-all-work responded with a slight shrug and a whisper: 'Student. Bogs, archaeology or something.'

'Or something?'

'Search me,' a more expansive, disinterested shrug this time. 'Old monuments, hieroglyphics, that sort of thing.'

'I see.' Goddard shifted his eyes away from the brunette. 'Maybe you can help me. I need some directions.'

'Certainly, if I can. By the way, my name is Murty.'

'Right Murty. Look, I'm trying to locate this fellow Arthur Leon. Do you know where he lives?'

The youth's eyes narrowed cautiously for a moment. 'Why do you want to know?'

'I'm a photo-journalist, Murty. I have to interview him for a magazine. That's all.'

'Everyone wants to interview him it seems.' Murty pouted.

'Everyone? What do you mean?'

'Yesterday Mr Medwin in room sixteen. A little while ago it was Miss Fontana in room fourteen. Suddenly everyone wants to know everything about Leon. And they keep asking me. Why me? I haven't had anything to do with — I haven't even spoken to that person in months!'

'Tell me about Miss Fontana. What did she want to know about Leon?'

'There's nothing to tell. Look Mr Goddard, I'm really very busy ....'

Goddard placed another two pounds on the counter: 'Have a drink on me.'

'Ta, but Mammy doesn't allow me to drink.'

'Keep it anyway. Now tell me about Miss Fontana.'

'There's nothing to tell. Honestly. She just wanted to know where she might find him. Leon, that is.'

'And you told her?'

'Why not? It's none of my business who goes up there.'

'You mentioned someone named Metcalfe?'

'Medwin. Room sixteen.'

'Okay, Medwin. Who's he?'

'An American gent.'

'Is he a journalist?'

'I don't think so.'

'What did he want to know about Leon?'

Murty shrugged. 'Just the usual Yankee tourist looking for cheap originals, that's all. He enquired about local artists, you know the sort of thing. The Yanks are culture mad, but they rarely recognise *real* talent even when it's right before their eyes.' Murty delicately flicked froth from the summit of the pint and then topped it up again until the foam was sliding down the glass in creamy tresses. With a pout he resumed: 'I wouldn't mind, Mr Goddard, but some of my very *best* seascapes are right here on the walls for everyone to see. And they're *all* for sale. Quite reasonable too. But Mr Medwin barely glanced at them. Some art lover, I must say!'

'So, you're an artist Murty?'

'From October to April I study art in Dublin. I only work here for Mammy in the summer months. In my spare time I get some painting done.' He nodded towards the bright daubs in the aluminium frames. 'As a photographer Mr Goddard — as a very experienced one, I'm sure — what do *you* think? Your honest opinion now.'

Goddard took a mouthful from the pint, and still with the tumbler in his hand, walked slowly across to the wall, pretending to examine the paintings with a knowing and critical eye. It was no time for honesty. Murty was much better at pulling pints than smearing canvasses. Goddard deliberately contrived his art scrutiny so that he ended up close by the brunette. 'What do you think?'

She raised large, dark eyes up to meet his but responded with a kind of absent-minded stare; 'Sorry?'

'The paintings, what do you think of them?'

She didn't even bother to look or to smile as she intoned 'very nice' and then returned to her books. Beautiful, especially the eyes! About twenty-eight, twenty-nine age-wise, Goddard opined. Then, with just a hint of a 'what-the-hell' shrug he returned to the bar where Murty was anxiously waiting.

'Nice, very nice,' Goddard nodded approvingly. 'You've got a good eye for colour Murty. Good composition too.'

'Do you *really* think so?' Murty smiled in deprecation of his skill.

'Sure. A very good eye for colour.'

'He said so too. Said I showed great promise. Arthur, I mean. He said I've an innate feeling for the subject and that I have a sensitive, delicate touch. That sort of thing. He's like that, Leon. All compliments and charming at first. But it's only an act.' This time the shrug and the pout had a miffed, disillusioned quality.

'How well do you know him?'

'Really Mr Goddard, you've just as many questions as Miss Fontana. Why is everyone so bloody interested in Arthur Leon? As a painter he's a has-been. And as a person he's — he's just *disgusting*.'

'In what way?'

'Never you mind. Curiosity killed the cat.'

'You answered Miss Fontana's questions, didn't you?'

'She only wanted to know how to get to Owls Watch.'

'Owls Watch?'

'Owls Watch Cottage. Leon's place.'

'And you told her?'

'Naturally. None of my business who goes up there.'

'Okay, so supposing you tell me.'

'Easy. You just go up the street, turn left where the street forks, go on for about a mile until you reach the trees, and then, where the road drops down towards the beach you'll see a white bungalow on the left. It looks out over the sea. That's it.'

'How long since Miss Fontana left?'

'About tweny — twenty-five minutes ago.'

'Thanks Murty.' Goddard finished the pint and pushed

himself off the bar stool.

'Are you going there?'

'Yeah. That's what they pay me for. Cheers.'

'Bye bye. Don't forget, dinner at eight to nine-thirty. And Mr Goddard —'

'Yeah?'

'Mind how you go.' Murty lowered his gaze and pursed his lips in a prim, disapproving fashion. 'Arthur Leon is a bum pincher, if you know what I mean?'

'Don't worry Murty. I used to be the college boxing champ.'

'Well if you have to punch him give him a good thump for me too.'

He sounded as if he meant it.

Goddard left the hotel and climbed up the steep main street. Where it petered out into a few old cottages at the summit, and where the road forked and the wind came scything in from all directions, he had a fairly good view of most of the island. It was more or less pear shaped, about three miles in length and about half that in breadth. The fat end of the pear was stuck out into the Atlantic and the narrow end faced the mainland with the harbour and the hotel at the very tip and closest to the mainland. There was no signpost at the fork in the road, and no real need for one. From his present vantage point at the top of the main street Goddard could see quite clearly how the road branched to right and left and followed the coastline on either side.

The right showed higher, more open ground, with only a few stunted trees that leaned inland against the harsh seawinds. There was the usual west of Ireland patchwork of tiny fields hemmed in by their rough stony walls and a sprinkling of cottages here and there in the distance. Beyond, at the farthest end of the island, blackish cliffs fell down to the sea. The left was more picturesque. It was fairly wooded in places, the land flowing gently down to some sandy beaches which could be glimpsed in places through the trees. Tomorrow maybe, he'd take the plate camera up here and get a few scenic transparencies. For the present he had his assignment to think about and Arthur Leon and, possibly, some journalistic competition from Gloria Fontana who seemed to have stolen a march on him.

Goddard took the left-hand turning as Murty had directed and for about a mile passed nice new expensive-looking bungalows and converted cottages with neat lawns and rockeries and gate signs with names like 'Seaview' and 'Tig-na-Mara' and 'Bayhaven'. Clearly this was the monied, holiday side of the island.

There were still a few hours of daylight left but grey torrents of cloud were already flooding the sky and darkening it ominously. The wind contained a few little spits of rain. Goddard zipped the anorak right up to his neck and increased his pace.

Twenty minutes later he found Owls Watch Cottage. It stood in a small clearing between larch and fir trees, an imitation hacienda of stone and timber with a little green apron of lawn tucked in around it.

He tried the front door bell a few times but when he got no answer he followed the crazy paving round to the back of the house, which was one long curved window running the entire length of the building. Facing south it must have caught every bit of sunlight on offer during the day and it looked out over the trees on the lower slope towards the bay and the mainland. But Goddard had no time to admire the view.

'Hello, anybody there?'

He moved along the glass wall until he reached a sliding door. It was partly open. 'Mr Leon? Hello, anyone at home?'

Goddard took a deep breath, slid back the door and entered. 'Hello?'

The first thing to confront him was a strikingly beautiful woman in the nude. She looked at him from a large canvas mounted on an easel, a dark-haired seductress in the pale slant of light from the overhead roof window. Although the work wasn't finished — only the head and shoulders and cleavage — the remaining lines and base colours and brush strokes hinted at a wanton, sensuous pose in the finished work. The dark, somnolent and provocative eyes reaching from the canvas invited him further into the room.

'Anybody home? Hello ... Mr Leon?'

He continued to study the painting as he edged diffidently forward through the chaos of canvases, work tables, palettes and brushes and tubes. Leon might be a sloppy worker but he was a damn fine painter. That much Goddard could see. The only incongruity was in the bottom left hand corner of the canvas. It was peppered with a pattern of curious little scorched holes. Now why did the painter need to do that?

The long crimson lips smiled teasingly as though the woman in the painting was finding secret amusement in Goddard's puzzlement.

No wonder she was smiling.

It was only when Goddard let his gaze travel down from the little scorch marks that he saw the artist's body lying on the floor to one side of the easel. His grey smock was daubed with all manner of paint wipings – blues and greens and orange and pink — but there was no mistaking the crimson mess that was still shiny damp on his chest. The blood was beginning to congeal around a similar pattern of little black scorch holes.

2

If Goddard had felt like throwing up in the instant of discovering a bloodied corpse no one would have noticed, because there was an awful mess of paint tubes, colours and daubs all over the parquet flooring. And Arthur Leon was lying in the middle of the mess. At least Goddard reckoned that's who it was. The dead man certainly fitted the description given to Goddard by his London editor – lean, handsome in a saturnine way, well-trimmed beard and moustache.

And now very much dead.

He was lying on his back, blasted into a spreadeagled position amongst a tumble of drawing sheets and pencils, a grey-tipped paint brush still clasped in his left hand, a long smear of the same greyish oil paint slashing down his right cheek and across his nose as if the brush had wiped across his face as he'd thrown up his arms and fallen backwards from the shotgun blast. Shotgun? Well, Goddard reckoned it must have been a shotgun at close quarters. Two barrels full, to judge from all those little pellet holes on the edge of the canvas and then a whole clatter of them sprinkling the dead man's chest and adding to the gory mess welling from it.

It was a sickening sight. After he'd quickly knelt down

and checked the wrist pulse in a forlorn hope of finding some vestige of life Goddard felt dry-mouthed and nauseous. He turned away and leaned over a drawing desk, holding his stomach. It must have been his professional eye for detail that had enabled him to take in everything at a glance, and even now, with his back to the corpse, to visualise everything with clarity. Up to this the only dead bodies he'd ever seen had been from a comparatively safe distance and they'd been nothing more gruesome than inert shapes under a blanket on a stretcher. And between Goddard and the dead there had always been ambulance men and fire officers and policemen to take charge of things ....

Police?

He'd have to ring the police immediately!

He was still squelching paint tubes underfoot and stumbling about in the debris in search of a phone when he heard the footsteps behind him. The faint, creaking noise made him jerk round in a half spin.

The blonde was edging in through the glass door.

'You'd better not come in ....!'

Goddard was too late. He saw her gaze travel quickly from his face to the dead man on the floor.

'Oh Jesus!' she said in a kind of tired, defeated whisper as she took a few hurried paces towards the body, then quickly recoiled, stepping back a few paces until she bumped into the nearest chair and sank down on it. 'Is he ... *dead?*'

''Fraid so. Hey, just in case you're getting any wrong ideas, I didn't do it. I just got here a few moments ago.'

'Poor bleedin' Arty,' she muttered, slowly shaking her head from side to side.

'I wanted to interview him and to shoot —'

'*Shoot?*'

'Not what you think. I'm a professional photographer

for Christ sake!' Goddard swore, whipping the Nikon from his pocket and proferring it by way of explanation. He was about to launch into an account of his purpose here until he realised that she wasn't listening. Her eyes kept shifting back towards the body.

'Poor bleedin' Arty.'

'Come on, I think we better phone the police.'

She wrenched her gaze from the corpse and looked directly at Goddard for the first time. 'Police?'

'Yes. We'll have to report this.'

The stunned look began to fade from her eyes: 'There's no phone.'

'How do you know that?'

'I tried to call him from the hotel before I came up here. The fairy told me that Arty wasn't on the phone.' She stood up, casting one more involuntary glance at the body. 'No phone, but if I know old Arty there'll be a bottle of gin close at hand. God, but I can use a stiff drink right now. How about you?'

Goddard was accustomed to social drinking. Somehow this seemed irreverent. Without actually letting his eyes settle on the body he indicated the dead man with a grim nod. 'What about him?'

'I don't think Arty has much of a thirst at the moment,' she said, either savagely bitter or suddenly resigned to the fact of his death. With unerring accuracy she quickly located the cocktail cabinet. Even in this unreal and macabre situation Goddard couldn't fail to notice the lithe gracefulness of her movements.

'On second thoughts,' she remarked, quite matter-of-factly, as she poured a generous measure of gin into a glass and dashed it with some lemon, 'if Arty's gone where I think he's gone, and where he certainly deserved to go, then he must have a million dollar thirst about now.'

'You knew him, I take it?' Goddard asked, following her.

'Yeah, I knew the creep.' She handed an empty glass to Goddard. 'Whiskey, gin, Vermouth or red plonk?'

'Is that a nice way to speak of the dead?' Goddard took the whiskey bottle and poured his own. Neat.

'I was referring to him when he was living. He was a worthless creep then. I'm sure he's still a creep, wherever he is.'

It was a strange feeling to be standing so close to her, each of them clutching a glass of liquor as if they'd just met at a cocktail party or a publicity reception, and all the while with a dead man lying just a few feet away.

'We'd better notify the police,' Goddard repeated after he tossed back most of the whiskey in one joyless gulp.

'Not until I find what I came for.'

'What's that?'

'None of your business. By the way, just what *is* your business here?'

'I told you. I'm a photo-journalist. I came here to interview him and to take some pictures.'

'I think someone just screwed up the interview bit, but what's keeping you with the pictures? That's what newspapers pay for isn't it? You've got a scoop here.'

'You're right, I suppose. It just didn't seem the proper thing to do.'

'If you're looking for permission from the next-of-kin you've got it.'

'You?'

'I'm his wife. Correction, ex-wife. Or widow, whatever.' She had lit a cigarette and with the glass still in her hand she began to rummage through the scattered papers littering the work desk.

'My condolences.'

'Yeah, thanks,' she murmured absently.

Now she was yanking out drawers and presses and hurriedly sifting through their contents. Her sense of urgency got to him. Goddard left down his glass and began to work the Nikon, snap-snapping away, moving expertly around the dead body and the painting on the easel, his mind suddenly in tune with the camera and click-clicking over the professional implications of such a scoop.

The blonde was still banging round the drawers and the cupboards and spilling out the contents of manilla folders and envelopes and sketch pads.

'Cut it out,' Goddard snapped. 'The police don't like things messed about and disturbed in a murder investigation.'

She turned and looked at him, her eyes neither hostile nor friendly. A little confused and anxious perhaps. 'Alright. You're a photographer. Where would a bloke like Arty keep a set of valuable photos?'

'You were married to him. You tell me.'

'I haven't seen Arty in almost seven years. Please, where would he keep such photos?'

'How would I know? In a safe maybe.'

'If we find one could you open it?'

'Are you mad! Listen, the police are going to put some very awkward questions to you and me. I've no intention of adding house breaking and safe cracking to their list. Now come on, let's get out of here!'

But the girl had already crossed the room and opened the door to a small annexe off the main bungalow. Goddard hurried over with the intention of restraining her — and then he halted in the doorway and gave a low, awe-filled whistle.

It was a compact studio, full of the most expensive and sophisticated photographic equipment that Goddard had ever seen. At a quick glance he was able to pick out such items as a Hasselblad with Biogen lens for wide-angle copying, a Japanese job for really high magnifications and another rigidly linked to a copying easel. There was an enlarger, the latest studio flash units, an elaborate wall-mounted opaque projector looking down onto a drawing table and another with a built-in drawing board and a hood to screen the working area from the room lighting. Goddard followed the girl in.

She was already busily turning over every scrap of paper and envelope and folder she could lay her hands on, eagerly searching and riffling through piles of photographs. Goddard didn't bother to stop her. He was too busy himself examining a whole shelf full of the usual dark room chemicals and another chock full of a lot of stuff that he'd never even heard of: a row of dusty looking jars with labels like *walnut oil, bone white, caput mortuum, cera colla* and other strange descriptions. These, with some very ancient looking brushes and painting knives and bits and pieces of dirty old canvas left him wondering if the place in reality was a painter's workshop or a photographer's studio. Both, maybe?

There was no safe, and no sign apparently of whatever photographs the girl was looking for. She had unearthed some pictures though.

'I don't believe it — Arty gone religious?'

The pictures were all full-colour reproductions of the exact same subject — an old-style Madonna and Child oil painting — and they all stared out from a dozen different books. Each was a splendidly printed art publication, mostly Italian and French, and no two editions were the same. Goddard checked them rapidly and saw that each one opened out on whichever page showed the same dark-haired Madonna with the same plump, cherubic, golden-haired Infant in her arms and he noted too that there was scarcely any colour variation between the various printed reproductions. Even when he switched on the projector the same Madonna, enlarged this time, came up on the drawing board.

'What does it mean? What's all this stuff?'

'I'm not sure,' Goddard muttered, still poking about. But he *was* sure of one thing; someone — almost certainly Leon — was not merely a painter who dabbled in photography, or a photographer who dabbled in paintings of Old Masters. All this high-powered equipment suggested something more sophisticated than dabbling. And Goddard knew enough to know that there was everything on hand here for expert copying. Forgery even?

'There's nothing here. I give up,' she said, suddenly defeated. She was leaning against the door jamb and pouting smoke from a fresh cigarette. 'Maybe you're right. We ought to get out of here.'

'Yes. We better notify the police,' Goddard intoned, switching his interest from the studio. He took her arm and led her out again into the other room, past the shattered body of her ex-husband, using his body to shield her wide-eyed gaze from the grisly sight.

'God, I never thought it was going to turn out like this,' she said in a low voice. Her eyes were remarkably clear, neither frightened nor tragic.

'Neither did I,' Goddard added grimly. 'I was just chasing a job of work.'

They slipped out through the glass door and followed the crazy paving back out to the lane. Overhead the rain was beginning to drip from a dark layer of cloud. The spatters were increasing and the wind had grown in strength so that it was now bending and twisting the young saplings and bushes skirting the lane. With each fresh gust of sea wind the foliage changed lustre. The ferryman had been right; a storm before the night was over. They hurried on down the lane.

When they reached the first bungalow they ran up to the door and Goddard jabbed an impatient forefinger on the buzzer until a huge, shadowy figure loomed up behind the frosted glass. The door was suddenly jerked open. It was the broken-nosed man with the crisp grey hair that they had both seen coming over on the boat earlier in the day.

'Do you have a phone?'

'Yes —'

'We need to use it. It's urgent.'

'Come in then. What's the trouble?' He glanced at each of them in turn and when the glare left his eyes they were not unfriendly.

'We've just come from Arthur Leon's place. He's dead.'

'*Dead*?'

Goddard nodded: 'And it looks like murder.'

Open-mouthed, the big fellow sketched a rapid Sign of the Cross on his forehead and chest.

'The phone please.'

'Yes. Yes of course. This way ....'

He lumbered quickly ahead of Goddard and the girl into a nicely furnished lounge, all the while shaking his massive head from side to side. 'Dead, you say? Good Lord, *murdered*? The police will have to be told.'

'That's why we're here.'

He grabbed the phone from where it rested on top of a low bookshelf and dialled. He nodded to Goddard and the girl to sit down.

'Hello? Hello, Jack Sweeney here. Is the sergeant there? When was that? ... No, then you'll have to come yourself, Sean ... immediately ... yes ... because I've two people here with me now that say they've just come from Owls Watch.... No, Owls Watch ... yes, the painter fellow ... yes, and they say he's been murdered ... that's what I said, *murdered* ....'

Sweeney glanced from Goddard to the girl for verification.

'... That's what they say Sean ... two of them, man and a woman.... What? ... I don't know ... strangers ... hotel guests, I think ....'

Again Goddard and the girl nodded in unison.

'... Yes ... yes, came over today on the ferry ... sure wasn't I on the same boat Sean ... yes, I was leaving Nellie over to the mainland to catch the Dublin bus .... Aye, and these two were on the return boat ....'

A pause. Sweeney looked at both of them in turn. 'He wants to know your names ....'

'Goddard. Joe Goddard, freelance photographer.'

'Gloria Fontana. Actress.'

Sweeney repeated the information.

'And he wants to know if you touched anything at Leon's cottage?'

'No,' Gloria cut in quickly and emphatically, stifling any admission Goddard may have intended to make.

Matters continued like this for another two minutes, with Sweeney acting as a kind of telephonic interpreter and relaying the answers into the mouthpiece. Finally, with a curt nod at the phone, he replaced it in its cradle and returned it to the bookshelf. 'He says that you're to wait here. He'll be here in a few minutes.'

'Who's *he*?' Gloria asked.

'Sean Muldowney. The local Garda.'

'It means policeman,' Goddard explained, remembering her Kensington background.

'Aye, and it's a rough thing for Sean and him just a few weeks short of his retirement. That and the fact that the sergeant returned to the mainland yesterday. You see we've never had a murder on the island before. I doubt if Sean Muldowney would properly know how to deal with that sort of an investigation. Dog licences and fishing permits and the odd drunken fight, that's about Sean's strength. A murder investigation,' Sweeney shook his head dubiously. Then, after a moment, he asked: 'Can you be certain it was murder?'

'If it wasn't murder it was a damn strange way to commit suicide.'

'Mr Leon was a damn strange individual,' Sweeney muttered, half to himself.

'How well did you know him?' Goddard asked.

'Me?' Sweeney looked up sharply. 'Not very well.' His careless shrug didn't quite conceal a hint of antipathy. Then, suddenly, and with an expansive wave of his hand, he offered: 'Can I get you anything? Tea or coffee maybe? I'm afraid I don't have anything stronger. I don't keep hard liquor in the house.'

'Coffee would be fine, thanks. I take it you didn't like Leon?'

'He wasn't an easy man to like. Few people hereabouts took to him.'

'Why was that?'

'Hard to say exactly. People hereabouts have a sayin' — "if you need to pluck nettles, then use a stranger's hand". That fellah Leon had a great knack of gettin' other folk to pluck nettles for him ....' From the open door of the kitchenette, where he was preparing the coffee, Sweeney continued: 'Meself, I spent upwards of thirty years pluckin' other people's nettles on the hard graft of London buildin' sites and labourin' work with little enough to sustain me save the hope of earnin' a sufficiency to ease me ould age. Herself and meself came back here to be buried among our own. But when the Gover'mint fellahs brought the electric to the island a few years back I took a notion of renovatin' a few of the ould cottages as holiday homes for the quality and Dublin folk. Includin' Owls

Watch, more's the pity. Because with the buildin' of it, and all them specifications about overhead windows for paintin' by, I'd neither the time nor the sense to be readin' all that small print. And that good-for-nothin' bastard Leon, who should've been tied to a cow's tail and scuttered to death — Oh, savin' your presence Miss! — when it came to payin' his bills, was so slow that he'd be a great messenger to send for Death.'

'Yeah,' Goddard muttered, 'only today he wasn't sending. He was receiving.' While Sweeney was clattering about the kitchenette and airing his grievances Goddard's eyes roved about the lounge. It fitted in with the potted biography emanating from the other room and with Goddard's picture of Sweeney as a hard-working, thrifty, tough, ill-done-by, not-too-sophisticated type. The sideboard was all sports trophies and football photos and newscuttings, the mantelpiece lined with pipe-racks, penknives and tobacco tins, and, above them, on the rough-stone chimney breast, there was an oblong glass case with a huge stuffed fish in it and two rows of heavy brass hooks holding some horizontally placed fishing rods.

'It wasn't just the matter of the money though,' Sweeney resumed as he came back in, balancing a tray that contained a coffee pot, sugar bowl, milk jug, cups and a plate of biscuits. 'It was the bad name he got for Owls Watch that turned me and most of the island people against him.'

'His wild parties?' Gloria Fontana prompted.

'Aye. During the summer season he'd have a lot of strange people visiting. Hippies and the like. Why even the priest had to speak from the pulpit one Sunday morning and warn our people to steer clear of Owls Watch. Didn't mention the house or Leon in so many words, mind you, but we all knew who he was alludin' to. There was many a rumour of dirty carry-on.'

Gloria looked at Goddard and explained: 'Arty always had this thing about drugs, booze and gang bangs.'

'You knew him as well?' Sweeney enquired, offering her the first cup.

'A long time ago. In London.'

'I see,' Sweeney muttered. Then, with the air of someone who suspects that he may have spoken out of turn, or have given away too much of his own feelings, he lapsed into silence.

The policeman arrived before they were half way through their coffee. With a murder investigation in the offing Goddard had vaguely anticipated a squad car screeching up, its siren blaring and roof light flashing. And, because he was directly involved by virtue of his having stumbled on the dead body — might even be involved as the chief suspect for all he knew! – he wasn't too sure whether he should feel relieved or disappointed when he saw, through the window, an elderly man in uniform climbing out of a rather dusty Ford saloon. There was nothing in the policeman's appearance or demeanour to instil confidence in his ability to quickly resolve the circumstances of Leon's death. His lean peasant features under the peaked cap were drawn downwards into a frown of perplexity and uncertainty. His walk up the garden path was a kind of agitated shamble, awkward and out of sync, the shoulders slumped, and the loose knee joints pointing out at a different angle to the shiny toecaps of his black boots.

Sweeney jumped from his chair and lumbered quickly out to meet the policeman at the front door. Goddard heard the door opening; then low, urgent, almost conspiratorial whisperings drifted inwards. Sweeney and the policeman seemed to spend an inordinate length of time muttering together. Their words were indecipherable, only the grim tone reached back into the lounge to touch Goddard and the girl.

They exchanged anxious glances.

'What do you think?' Gloria asked.

'We found the body,' Goddard shrugged. 'We're going to have a lot of explaining to do.'

Sweeney led the policeman into the lounge and made brief, unnecessary introductions. The policeman managed not to notice Goddard's outstretched hand. Quickly and perfunctorily he went over many of the questions which he had just recently put to Goddard and the girl via Sweeney's phone. They gave him the same answers, monosyllabic and to the point.

'Right. Before we go into any further questions I think we should get up to Owls Watch and take a look at the scene of the crime while there's still enough light. Never know what we might find.'

It proved to be a vain hope. After they had all quit Sweeney's bungalow and were getting into the car the policeman suddenly exclaimed: 'What the hell is that?'

All eyes followed his startled gaze in the direction of Owls Watch. Goddard saw thick whorls of black smoke rising above the trees. Every few seconds spurts of flame and a shower of sparks leaped into the air, rending and lighting up the pall of smoke.

'The cottage is on fire!'

'Come on. Quick!'

It only took minutes to race back up the lane — and only seconds in which Goddard's trained eye briefly glimpsed a dark-haired woman in a yellow windcheater and what seemed to be a darkish tweed skirt ambling slowly across the high moorland about a mile off to his right. Suddenly she was lost from view. Had the others noticed her? Who was she — the studious young brunette with the books and the Gaelic coffee? Before the questions had even begun to form in Goddard's mind the old sedan screeched to a halt at the gate to Owls Watch and he had the back door already open. Sweeney and the policeman were right behind him as he flung open the gate and started across the lawn. But by then they could all see that it was too late. The whole place was engulfed in flames. Whipped up by the strong winds the fire was racing across the roof, and through the frightening brilliance of the windows they could see long and vivid tongues of flame licking across the oaken beams. They tried to get to the front door but the heat was intense and drove them back. Goddard hurried round to the rear of the house. It was just as bad. Worse.

Through the long glass window he had a better, more horrifying view of the extent of the inferno. There was no sign of the corpse or the easel or the drawing tables — nothing but a mass of flame filling the entire ground area and streaking up the walls. There was a great crackling noise and then a crash as part of the ceiling collapsed. Goddard stepped back from the great blasts of heat and just stood there for a few seconds, silent and helpless and mesmerised by the awful destruction. He was quickly joined by Sweeney and the policeman, Muldowney.

'Hi there! Hi you guys!'

It was some moments before Goddard noticed a tubby little man struggling up from the direction of the lower trees and the beach. He was waving his arms frantically. He came clambering up, panting to a halt and joining Goddard and the others as they backed out across the lawn from the threat of heat-shattered glass.

'*Jeez*! That's sure some bonfire. Anybody hurt?'

'No.'

'Well I guess that's something to be thankful for.'

Goddard turned. The newcomer had to be an American — the gum-chewing, the blue-and-white baseball cap, the yellow windcheater, the red-and-white checkerboard slacks pushed down into rubber wading boots. He had a sea-angler's rod in one hand and a net catch-bag over his shoulder. He was middle-aged and sweating profusely from his uphill exertions.

'Name's Medwin. Hank Medwin.' The accent clinched it. 'I was down on the shore getting in some fly-fishing. Suddenly I hear this kinda whoosh sound and then all this black smoke comes tumbling out over the trees. Jeez, some bonfire. Anybody in there?'

Nobody answered. The American followed Goddard and Sweeney and Muldowney back round to the front of the burning cottage. Gloria Fontana was just inside the front gate, hesitant and edging back from the great waves of heat.

Medwin wasn't the only newcomer to arrive on the scene. Just as they were all beginning to congregate in a little knot on the lawn and wondering what to do next a large flashy estate car came roaring up the lane, lurching and swaying against the grass margins of the ditches. Its occupants were spilling out of opposite doors even before it scrunched to a halt.

First out was a girl — about eighteen or nineteen years of age, her slim figure encased in black sweater, grey jodhpurs and sleek riding boots, her blonde ponytail hair streaming out behind her in the wind — and with a sobbing cry she started running towards the cottage. But the driver was out of his seat just as fast and, despite his beefy frame and a waist thickening with middle-age, he was rounding the nose of the car and catching up with her at the gate. He grabbed her roughly by the arm.

'Let go — *please!*'

'Take it easy Karen —'

'Let go, damn you!' The girl screamed. 'Let go of me! Arthur may be in there —'

'Karen! Stop it!' He had a firm, commanding presence. And an even firmer hold on her arm.

As the girl struggled and twisted against him they were quickly joined by the third occupant of the car. Like the beefy, middle-aged man the third occupant was expensively dressed and looked somewhere in the forties. She was black-haired and very beautiful and ....

And Goddard recognised her instantly as the nude model for the canvas Leon had been working on. There was no mistaking the same long crimson lips and the dark somnolent eyes. Only now the lips and the eyes and the darkly provocative features were frozen into a stunned expression as the woman stared at the giant flames belching through the roof and the shattered windows.

Her eyes, still glazed with shock, turned on the policeman: 'Arthur — where's Arthur?'

'I'm very sorry Mrs Sefton,' Muldowney intoned, removing his cap mournfully and stepping towards her. 'I'm afraid that Mr Leon is —' his eyes flitted towards the inferno for just a fraction of a second. 'But if it's any consolation to you ma'am, Mr Leon was already dead before the house caught fire.'

'Dead?' With a dull uncomprehending stare the dark eyes went back to the blazing cottage. 'Dead — Arthur?'

'*Dead!*' The ponytailed girl echoed in a hysterical scream. 'Dead ... oh no! *No!*'

Shrieking like a mad woman she tore herself from the man's hold and flung herself at the older woman. 'You bitch! You ... it's your fault! You did it!'

She was clawing viciously at the other woman's face. '*You jealous old bitch! You killed —*'

The man came up quickly behind her, swung her round, and brought the back of his hand hard across her face. 'Shut up!'

'Can't you see Daddy — she was jealous of Arthur and

me! She —'

'That's enough Karen! You are distraught.'

'And you're blind!' The girl was still struggling and sobbing. 'Blind fool! Behind your back she was having it off with Arthur until he fell in love with me! He loved me ... *Me*! And then she —'

'Shut up Karen!' He silenced her anguished words with another sharp backhander. Then he dragged her over to the estate wagon, wrenched open the door, bundled her into the back seat, and slammed the door. Pocketing the car keys he hurried back to the older woman. She was still standing stark and immobilised and staring dully at the fire and seemingly unaware of the clawed nail marks on her cheeks. The man placed his arm protectively about her shoulder.

'Come dear. There's nothing we can do here.'

But she just shrugged her shoulder out from under his arm and stepped away.

'Helen, please.'

'Damn you Jack. Just leave me alone.' With one final, painful, backward glance at the burning cottage she walked away and went over and stood by the door of the car. But her dark eyes were without tears.

The beefy, floridly handsome man gave the briefest suggestion of a hapless shrug and turned, frowning, to the policeman.

'As you can see Sean, both my wife and my daughter are quite — well, quite overcome by this shocking tragedy. I think I should get them home immediately.'

'Perfectly understandable Mr Sefton.'

'You may phone me at the Laurels should you need me for anything.'

'Thank you sir, but I don't think that will be necessary.'

'Very well then,' Sefton, smiling in a cold bland way, glanced over at the estate car. Then he abruptly swung his gaze around to include Goddard, Sweeney and Gloria Fontana, and gave a curt apologetic bow. 'I must ask you to excuse this unfortunate little scene. My family are quite upset, as you can imagine. Arthur — Mr Leon — was a close friend and neighbour.'

Sefton, grey-templed and impressive, turned smartly and stomped over to the car.

Seconds later the big station wagon was swinging round in a short vicious arc and spewing up a screech of fresh gravel from the lane's surface. Then it was roaring off again.

'Lovely family,' Gloria Fontana whispered, sidling up close to Goddard. 'Christmas dinner must be a real get-together with Daddy and Mummy and Baby daughter.'

Muldowney, catching them together in a protective huddle from the wind and the increasing blasts of rain on the one hand, and the fiery blasts of heat on the other, put his cap back on his bald head and trudged over to them.

'When you found the body, when you were in there earlier, did either of you notice if there was a fire lighting in the house?'

'No.'

'No, there wasn't any fire.'

'An electric fire maybe?'

Trying to remember, Goddard and Gloria looked at each other and then shook their heads.

'Could either of you have left a burning cigarette down somewhere?'

'No. No cigarette,' Gloria said rather abruptly, neither looking at Goddard or giving him time to contradict her.

But in that moment Goddard had an instant vision of her standing beside Leon's drink cabinet with a gin glass in one hand and a cigarette in the other. And another glimpse of her standing against the door jamb of the little studio puffing a fresh cigarette just before they'd left the place. Christ, with all that film and paper and dark room material the whole place would go up like a bomb if she'd carelessly tossed her cigarette end away!

Carelessly — or deliberately?

She'd certainly been very concerned about some photographs, enlisting his support in a frantic search. And then just as suddenly she'd given up her search. Why? What sort of photographs? If she'd wanted to locate the pictures and then destroy them then what better way to ensure their destruction than by tossing a lighted cigarette into one of the waste baskets?

And what better way of destroying all the clues pointing to the circumstances — and the perpetrator — of Leon's gruesome death?

3

The fury of the storm rattled and shook the windows of Muldowney's tiny office. On the dark panes the rain sizzled and streamed down in heavy shimmering rivulets. Muldowney, behind the desk, tried the phone once more, dialling, listening and then returning it to its cradle with a gesture of futility.

'Dead. It happens every now and again whenever we get one of these storms.' He settled back in his creaky swivel chair. 'I'll go up to the Laurels later. Mr Sefton has a two-way radio.'

Goddard and Gloria Fontana sat opposite him, both silent, waiting for the photos to arrive. Muldowney, glancing once more at the open page of the notebook before him on the desk, had run out of questions for the time being. Goddard reached for another cigarette and mentally reviewed the situation.

The policeman had gone over the same ground again and again, probing, re-phrasing his questions, neither patently hostile nor accusative, but slowly paring everything down to a few simple facts: both Miss Fontana and Mr Goddard, strangers, had arrived on the island for the very first time that day — the very day that Mr Leon had been murdered by person, or persons, unknown — and, to all intents and purposes, Miss Fontana and Mr Goddard were the only people to have visited Owls Watch that day. They were the chief, probably the only, suspects. The very simplicity of the situation made it all the more formidable.

And the steady, relentless tenor of Muldowney's interminable questions had gradually effected a kind of coalition between Goddard and the girl, an affinity, a vague conspiracy of reticence in which neither volunteered the information of her cigarette smoking at the scene of the crime, of her eager search for some pictures, or of the discovery of Leon's curious studio with all its sophisticated equipment. If the elderly, quietly spoken and seemingly slow-thinking policeman had settled on them as the most convenient suspects then neither Goddard nor Gloria Fontana had felt disposed to assist him with any gratuitous data.

And Goddard was in no doubt that he was a suspect. That much was obvious from the fact that when he had freely offered his roll of film as the only tangible proof to date of the crime — the fire had gutted the cottage and the corpse — Muldowney hadn't allowed Goddard to process the negatives and print them. That task had been handed over to the local chemist from the dusty suntan lotion shop two doors down from the police station. Goddard had been denied the thrill of seeing his pictures swimming into focus under the enlarger. Why? Did Muldowney think he might destroy or alter some vital piece of evidence?

'Can we go now?' the girl suddenly asked.

Muldowney's lean face was all polite attention. 'I was hoping you might wait until the photographs got here. Until I can phone the sergeant and he can get the forensic lads down from Dublin it looks like only the two of you can help me with them.'

'Only us? Why haven't you brought in some of the others for questioning?' Goddard snapped, his voice so sharp that all eyes turned on him.

'Who, for instance?'

'Anyone. Anyone here on the island who owned a shotgun or who may have had a reason for killing Leon.'

'Lots of men hereabouts own a shotgun. But I can't think of anyone who'd have reason to —'

'Can't you? How about that fellow Sweeney? He lives very close to Owls Watch.'

'Jack?' Muldowney shook his head in quiet disbelief. 'What motive would he have?'

'Try this: Leon owed him a lot of money and was refusing to pay.'

'That's no motive. Half the people on the island owe money to Jack Sweeney and there's none in a hurry with payment. No, Mr Goddard, that motive would never stand up.'

'Okay, then how about that American guy Medwin? What was he doing hanging around the scene of the crime?'

'He said he was down on the beach. Fishing.'

'Yeah? Well he's no fisherman,' Goddard retorted. 'Have you ever heard of fly-fishing from a beach? That's what he said, fly-fishing. And from what little I know fly-fishing is for rivers, not for seashores. So that seems very suspicious to me.'

'I noticed that too,' Muldowney nodded, eyeing Goddard in what seemed to be a new light. 'The island people have a saying to the effect that a person often ties a knot with his tongue that he can't loosen with his teeth. You may depend that I'll be looking into all the knots.'

'And while you're at it,' Gloria Fontana added, 'you might look into the matter of those Sefton women.'

'What about them?'

'They were acting very strange and —'

'The Sefton family were friends of the late Mr Leon. Perhaps it's to be expected that they'd take his death rather badly.'

'Oh sure, very friendly,' Gloria said through a sarcastic veil of fresh tobacco smoke. 'Anyone could see that both the daughter and the mother —'

'Step-mother,' Muldowney corrected with all the pedantic exactitude of the law.

'... Step-mother and daughter were having it off with Arty.'

'Having it off?'

'Nookey. Sex. An affair. Call it what you like.' Gloria stubbed her cigarette into the ashtray with exasperation. 'They were all at it. I'd advise you to look into that side of things.'

Again the policeman nodded calmly: 'We've an old Irish saying, Miss Fontana, "it's a bad man who doesn't take advice, and a thousand times worse the man who takes everyone's advice".' From his pocket he took a pipe and tobacco pouch. 'Meanwhile, you two are the only people to claim to have actually *seen* the corpse and, in your case Mr Goddard, to have photographed the scene. That's why I'd appreciate it if you'd both stay and help me go over the photographs.'

At that moment, as though in league with the policeman, there was a swift rap on the door and then it was immediately opened from outside. A little fat man, bespectacled and moustached, came dripping in, his long raincoat and galoshes gleaming with rain.

'Ah, Michael John. Good.'

'There you are, Sean. Best I could do,' said the fat man, handing a large manilla envelope across the desk to the policeman and eyeing Goddard and the girl from under the streaming canopy of his umbrella. 'Anything further that —?'

'No. Thanks Michael John. That'll be all.'

The fat man paused in the business of lowering and closing the umbrella. 'One or two of the enlargements are a big fuzzy but —'

'Thanks Michael John. That'll be all. Don't worry, you'll be mentioned in despatches to the sergeant.'

'Right so.' Michael John backed reluctantly towards the door, the umbrella neither furled nor unfurled, nodding to Goddard and the girl and lingering for an invitation to have his whetted curiosity satisfied. 'If you are quite sure that there's nothing more ...?'

'Good night, Michael John,' the policeman said with an air of brusque finality, standing up.

As the door was closed behind the fat little chemist Muldowney mumbled: 'A person in whom God didn't put any sense, you can't beat it into him with a big stick.' Then he cleared a number of papers to one side of his desk and gently spilled the contents of the manilla envelope onto the clean surface. 'Now then, let's see what we have here. Go ahead, Mr Goddard.'

In some crazy way Goddard felt almost certain that the photographs would further point to his guilt in Muldowney's eyes. He knew that there were often deceptions in photos that people sometimes took for truth. Shadows and light and blurred backgrounds could distort and lie. He picked them up clumsily, first riffling through them for content and quality.

'These were taken with a synchronised flash, so they're a bit flat. I don't have any experience at forensic photography, but normally for this kind of thing, police photos, the lighting should be scientifically controlled. These were the best I could get under the circumstances.'

Goddard could see that there was no prize-winning

stuff among the shots, neither in the way he'd taken them nor in the way they'd been blown up, but they told their story nonetheless. It was all there, from every angle — long shots, close-ups, the victim front face and left and right profiles, everything in focus — the corpse sprawled among the sheets of drawing paper and pencils and paint tubes, the paintbrush still clasped in the left hand, the long smear of oil paint on his right cheek and the bridge of his nose, the pattern of pellet holes and the crimson mess on the front of his smock, more pellet holes on the bottom corner of the canvas, and the nude study of Mrs Sefton smiling sensuously from her perch on the easel. Every picture told a story of sorts and hinted strongly of the painter busy before the canvas, then surprised by an intruder, a brief tussle, a shotgun blast at point blank range. It was all there. Except who pulled the trigger. Goddard examined each photo in turn before handing them over to Muldowney, all the time half expecting to come across some inexplicable self portrait of himself aiming a shotgun instead of a camera.

'As I said, the lighting could be better. For this kind of thing it needs to be scientifically controlled,' Goddard said, rather apologetically.

'Let's take a look,' Muldowney said, slowly fingering blackish tobacco from the pouch into his pipe. 'Though it's been my experience over the years that solutions to the deepest mysteries lie not so much in physical clues — you know, print smears, ballistics, photos, that sort of thing — but in the hearts and minds of people. Still ....'

'What are we looking for exactly?' Gloria asked.

'I'm not sure,' Muldowney admitted. 'Clues, I suppose. It's with small stones that castles are built.'

'You've got to give him credit,' Gloria whispered in Goddard's ear as she pressed closer, looking over his shoulder at some of the pictures spread out on the desk.

Despite his preoccupation with the shots Goddard liked the feeling of her nearness, liked the faint perfume and the momentary, gentle pressure on his shoulder.

'Very often a murder victim tries to leave some indication as to the identity of the attacker. A sign of some sort.' Muldowney slowly moved a large magnifying glass back and forward between his nose and one of the pictures. Then he straightened up, rubbed his eyes and handed the glass to Goddard. 'Maybe you might spot something.'

'Nothing,' Goddard mumbled, his forefinger riffling through the shots and re-arranging them once more on the desk top. 'Nothing. Only what's there. Just like it was.'

Gloria had edged even closer to him, trying to peer down with him through the magnifying glass. Her thigh was actually brushing his. He deliberately tilted the glass in such a way that she had to press even closer to him. Then he felt her grow suddenly tense.

'Hey, wait a minute.' She snatched up one of the pictures. 'There's something about this one. Something missing or ... I don't know what, but something just doesn't seem right.'

'What?' Goddard coaxed.

'Take your time Miss Fontana. Take your time.'

'Yeah, now I have it. Arty is holding the paintbrush in his left hand, isn't he?'

Goddard checked to see that the print hadn't been reversed. 'Yes, that's right.'

'No. It's wrong. Arty was a right hander. He never used the left. Never. Couldn't even scratch his backside with it. And *always* the right for drawing and painting. Always. So why is he holding the brush in his left hand now?'

'Are you sure?'

'Positive. I was married to him for five years wasn't I?'

Goddard turned to Muldowney. 'Do you think it means anything? Could that be the clue, the sign, that you're looking for?'

'Maybe. Maybe not.' Muldowney turned the matter over in his mind for a few seconds. 'Could be sheer coincidence of course. Maybe he switched hands to wipe the brush or something. Then again he could have been trying to leave a sign as to who his killer was.'

'A left handed man?'

'Or a woman.'

'I'm right-handed,' Gloria grinned tautly.

'So am I,' Goddard added.

'I've already noticed that in both cases,' Muldowney said matter-of-factly as he once again spread and rearranged the photos on the desk. 'See anything else?'

Goddard shook his head. Gloria studied the pictures for a few moments and shrugged. 'No, nothing. Can we go now? I'm tired.'

'And I'm hungry,' Goddard said, reaching for his damp anorak and her trenchcoat.

'Yes, of course,' Muldowney stood up, came round the desk and saw them to the door. 'If I need you again I'll know where to find you.'

'Sure,' Goddard agreed with a grim nod. There was no mistaking the policeman's meaning. In this storm there was no way off the island. If Muldowney suspected himself or Gloria — even if Muldowney had all the evidence necessary for a conviction! — he didn't have to formally charge them or lock them up. The island was a prison.

''Night Mrs Leon. Mr Goddard.'

'Good night.'

When the door snapped shut after them the elderly policeman returned to his swivel chair. A murder was scattered on the desk top for his inspection. It was all there — except for the photo that really mattered. The photo of the killer. He lit his pipe and picked up the magnifying glass once more. 'It's an old saying and a true one,' he muttered through the pipe clench, nodding his head with a quiet certitude, 'time is a good story-teller.'

Outside the storm was everywhere. It came shrieking up from the little stone harbour and down from the dark hills, great gusts of wind-driven rain that plastered Goddard and the girl closer together as they stumbled across the street to the hotel. She was clutching his arm for support and leaning her face down behind the bulwark of his shoulder.

'It's obvious that cop isn't looking any further than you and me Joe,' she said, the wind yelping around her and snatching the words away almost.

'Yeah, and with all his homespun philosophy and damn proverbs he's no bloody fool!'

Goddard really wanted to say that it had nothing to do with him, that he'd accidentally stumbled on the body, that he'd never known Leon before, that he'd no motive for killing; he wanted to ask her about her reason for coming here, and what was so special about the pictures she'd been searching for and if she accidentally — or deliberately? — tossed away a burning cigarette end at the cottage. He wanted to know if she'd killed Leon. But something in the way she clutched his arm and had just intoned his name — something told him this wasn't the time or the place. Later, maybe.

No, not *maybe*. Definitely!

The front door of the hotel was unlocked, but closed over against the fury of the storm. The interior was almost in semi-darkness. He steadied the girl as her high heels slithered wetly on the parquet flooring.

'Hey there, you guys! Been waitin' for you. Fancy an

aperitif before chow?' It was Medwin's voice coming loudly from the little cocktail lounge across from the shadowy reception area. He was ensconced on a tall stool at the bar, his short fat legs dangling a few inches from the floor. 'Whaddya say, you two? Like to buy you a drink. Kinda rough day, huh?'

The log fire and the muted lanterns above the bar looked cosy and inviting after the austerity of the one-roomed police station. Goddard took the girl by the arm before she could demur. 'Don't mind if we do. Thanks. It's a lousy night out there.'

Instead of Murty there was a big stout woman serving behind the bar. She had the same concertina of curls haloing her still pretty face, though unlike Murty's reddish tresses these were yellow and brassy. Goddard surmised that this must be Mammy.

'And you must be Miss Fontana and Mr Goddard,' she smiled maternally, plump elbows and massive bosom splaying out over the polished counter. 'My son told me. Rooms twelve and fourteen, isn't it? Terrible business today at Owls Watch, wasn't it? Still, it could've happened at the height of the season, and then where would we be? Be thankful for small mercies I always say. It will have all blown over by next season, thank heavens. Poor Murty was so upset at the tragedy that I gave him a few hours off duty, God help him.'

Medwin, still perched on his bar stool, swayed closer to Goddard and, just out of earshot, mumbled: 'Seems the kid and the dead guy were very buddy-buddy. Know what I mean? The kid took the news real bad. Gone to his room with a few tranquillisers, or somethin'. Ma's runnin' the bar.' In a much louder tone he continued: 'Okay, so what's is to be?'

'Gold Label please.'

'Something hot,' Gloria smiled wanly, settling herself

on the stool next to Goddard's.

'Got that Ma? Goldilocks and, say a Gaelic coffee. Okay?'

'Okay. Thanks.' Gloria pulled off her damp headscarf and put it in her trenchcoat pocket.

'So then,' Medwin turned back to Goddard, his bland smooth features breaking into a solicitous smile, 'J. Edgar Hoover give you a rough time over there?'

Goddard shook his head. 'Just a few routine questions.'

'No kiddin', huh?' He switched his smile to Gloria. 'How about you Miss Fontana?'

'Just routine. That's all.'

'Routine, huh? Good. Good. I'm glad to hear it.' He was still smiling affably, though the smile was having some difficulty reaching his eyes. He lowered his voice just a little, matching it to the movement of leaning slightly closer to Goddard. 'Real glad. 'Cause, you see, the talk round here is that as you two kids found the, eh, the deceased, and that as you're total strangers in this neck of the woods — well the talk is that you're kinda the number one suspects.'

Goddard spun round: 'Listen here Medwin —'

'Call me Hank. And take it easy kid. Look, I'm a stranger in these parts too, remember. I'm on your side. And I figure I could be in a position to help you folks.'

'I don't recall either of us asking for help.'

'Maybe not. But you're sure as hell gonna need it. 'Specially when that dumb cop over there hands the investigation over to the homicide guys. This storm ain't gonna last forever, you know. Come tomorrow and this sod of turf is gonna be crawlin' with cops. Professionals. Real hot shots.'

'Look, Mr Medwin —'

'Hank.'

'Look, I'm sure you mean well. But what's your interest

in all this?'

'Like I said, I wanna help.'

'How?'

'By doin' some good ole fashion horse tradin'. You give me some information, I give you some information.'

'What sort of information?'

'Well, for starters, what exactly did the cop wanna know?'

'I told you, just routine questions.'

'Routine like what did you find at Owls Watch before the joint went up in flames, or routine like what was your connection with Leon?' As he handed the drinks around, Gloria first, then Goddard, he proferred the glasses with his left hand. Goddard wondered if Gloria noticed it too.

'Cheers.' Goddard raised his glass. 'You mentioned horse trading. What have you got to offer?'

'Hah,' Medwin grinned, raising a mildly admonitory forefinger and gently shaking his head. 'You still haven't told me anythin' yet.'

'That makes us quits.'

A little silence began to build up. Medwin sipped his Scotch gingerly and then wiped his mouth inelegantly with the back of his hand. 'Unnerstand you took some pictures up there?'

'That's how I make my living.'

'Got them with you?'

Goddard shook his head. 'The policeman has them.'

'They show anythin' interestin'?'

'Why don't you call over to Muldowney in the morning? He might let you take a look at them.'

'Yeah, I might just do that.' He could see that he was getting nowhere with Goddard so, after another sip, he turned and beamed his kindly uncle smile on Gloria. 'Miss Fontana — or should I say Mrs Leon?'

Gloria shrugged, indifferent rather than discourteous.

'My condolences Mrs Leon. Musta been a tragic shock for you.'

'Yeah, but not nearly as tragic as being married to the bastard.'

'Like that, huh? Tell me about your late husband.'

'Another time maybe,' Gloria feigned a yawn. 'I'm hungry. I'd like to get out of these wet clothes and take a shower before dinner. Thanks for the drink Mr Medwin.'

'Call me Hank.' He made an expansive gesture with his plump little hands. 'Howsabout you Goddard, same again?'

'No thanks. I need to change for dinner too.' Goddard signalled to Murty's mammy who was down at the far end of the bar polishing a goblet. 'Another Scotch for Mr Medwin.'

'Skip it. I'll take a rain check.'

'Whatever you say.'

'See you folks at dinner?'

They were moving away from the bar and except for a swift, non-commital smile from Gloria they didn't answer.

'Ciao, anyway,' Medwin called after them.

On the way up the stairs Gloria murmured: 'He's left-handed. Did you notice?'

'Yes. And he's no fisherman either.'

'He was certainly fishing for a lot of information just now.'

'Which suggests that he's no ordinary harmless little tourist.'

'Right. So what's his interest in all of this?'

'A more important question right now,' Goddard said, pausing at the top of the stairs, 'is whether you might care to join me for dinner?'

She flashed a quick appreciative smile. 'That would be nice. Thanks Joe.'

'What time?'

'Eight thirty?'

'Fine.' Then she quickly leaned over and kissed his cheek. 'Thanks for everything Joe.'

And then she was gone, moving gracefully down the corridor to her room.

Goddard let himself into his own room. The wind and the unremitting rain snarled and slashed at the opposite window, shrouding everything of the outside world in dark mystery. He found the light switch and with a swift jab dissolved the darkness.

But not the mystery.

He wondered if he wasn't getting in too deep with Gloria?

4

Goddard stood under a hot shower for about ten minutes. Outside the storm was still howling and the windows were rattling and creaking. So were his thoughts. He was the only person on this stupid little island who was positive that he hadn't killed Leon. And before the phones were fixed and the storm abated he was going to have to come up with the name and the identity of the real killer. But who? In a thick lather of soap he stood there, rubbing his torso, going over the day's events and making out his own list of suspects. He started by eliminating the ferryman, the fat chemist and Guard Muldowney. Then he came to Sweeney. Could he have killed Leon because of the money owed to him? Hardly a motive for murder. Besides, Sweeney seemed more like the type who would have finished Leon off with his outsize fists rather than a firearm. Still, Goddard was in no hurry to cross him off his list.

Then came the Seftons. Which one? The wife, because Leon had switched his attentions to the step-daughter? Or the step-daughter because Leon was two-timing her by continuing to play around with the step-mother? Did the sexy painting have anything to do with that? Or maybe it was the husband, who may have discovered the painting and that Leon was screwing both of his women? That made sense, didn't it? The jealous husband and outraged father angle. Vengeance on the double. That figured. But if so, then where did the left-handed phoney fly-fisherman fit in? And if Leon was bisexual then maybe Murty the pretty maid-of-all-work had to be added to the equation. Why not? The jilted boyfriend, bitchily jealous of Leon's prowess as a painter and a philanderer? It was possible. Anything was possible. So now Goddard had a gay angle to add to the eternal triangle. And all the angles were beginning to jangle through his thoughts as he turned off the shower and reached for a towel.

And deep down he knew that he was deliberately going over and over this small list of suspects because he didn't want to consider the most obvious one. Gloria. He hated the idea but it kept recurring.

He hadn't mentioned to Muldowney that she'd set out for Owls Watch twenty minutes before Goddard had left the hotel nor had he mentioned anything about her frantic search for some incriminating photos. Twenty minutes before him. And yet she'd arrived a few minutes after him. Or so she claimed. But just suppose she had arrived first — she certainly had enough time! — and had demanded the photos in question, then quarrelled violently with an ex-husband whom she clearly detested, and then he'd started to threaten her or to rough her up and she'd grabbed out at the nearest weapon, say a loaded shotgun on the mantelpiece or something — there could have been one, Goddard hadn't looked — and then she blasted him to smithereens and dropped the weapon (it could easily have been lying amidst the chaos of drawing papers on the floor for all Goddard knew) and then she'd heard him at the front door, panicked, slipped out the back way, hid in the trees until Goddard came round the back and stumbled on the corpse, and then made her 'innocent' reappearance so that she could resume her search for the photos. Supposing all that had actually happened. It made sense, didn't it? Even down to Goddard's eagerness to contact the police, foiling her search for the pictures, and then how her chain smoking of cigarettes gave her the sudden inspiration to throw a lighted match or a cigarette butt in say a wastepaper basket — maybe that time when she was searching Leon's bedroom and Goddard was in the little studio? — yes, a red hot flash of brilliance that would effectively destroy its contents: corpse, shotgun, fingerprints, the mysterious and damning photographs. The lot. It made sense.

And maybe Medwin was right when he said that Goddard was a number one suspect. The patsey. The fall guy. And maybe that's what the blonde meant when she kissed his cheek and murmured 'Thanks for everything Joe'.

Goddard was almost finished dressing when his thoughts were interrupted by a swift *rat-tat-tat* on the door. Gloria?

'Come in.'

To his surprise, and disappointment, Medwin entered hurriedly with a broad grin trying to pass itself off as an apology.

'What do you want?' Goddard snapped.

'Sorry for the intrusion, but like I said, maybe a bit of horse-trading? Okay? Downstairs, awhile back, I figured maybe you didn't want to open up too much in front of Mrs Leon —?'

'Leave her out of this.'

'Whatever you say,' Medwin maintained the half-grin and raised his hands, palms outwards. 'Just take it easy Goddard, okay? Look, all I want is to pool our information and —'

'What makes you think I've any information to pool or horse-trade?'

'Good question. Let's just say that you tell me everything you saw, or found, today at Owls Watch before the joint went up in flames and I'll do the same. I'll level with you, Goddard. Right down the line. And I'll help you and the broad beat this murder rap. Okay?'

'Leave her out of this.'

'Chrissakes Goddard! Start thinking with your head 'stead of your genitals! The way things stand just now the local fuzz can nail you on a half-dozen charges.'

'Such as?'

'Awh, don't give me any of that "such as" shit! Just lissen to me. This guy Muldowney already has you and Mrs Leon down as number one suspects. By tomorrow, when they get these phones operating again or when the ferry is able to put out to sea, you're goin' to have some hot-shot murder squad guys combin' this island and takin' over the entire investigation. For you, kid, that's when it's really goin' to hit the fan.'

'Why me?' Goddard knotted his tie angrily. 'Why not someone else? For all anyone knows maybe *you* killed Leon!'

'Yeah, and maybe the Pope's got a harem. Cut the crap Goddard.' Medwin sighed wearily as he settled his bulky frame down on the side of the bed. From his jacket pocket he fished out a small plastic identity disk and handed it to Goddard. 'Now I'm gonna ask you, nice and easy, do you wanna do business?'

Goddard looked from the photo on the disk back to Medwin. It was him alright. *Henry J. Medwin. Chief Field Officer. Benwood Detective Agency.* New York address. Coast to coast and international affiliates, etcetera. Handing back the disk he asked: 'So, what's your interest in Leon?'

'Not Leon specifically. Leastways not now that he's dead. It's Sefton I'm after.'

'For murder?'

'Maybe, though I doubt it.' Medwin returned the identity disk to his pocket. 'For the past three-four years I've been on his trail and tryin' to tie him into some hefty art swindles. I'm actin' for a group of wealthy US clients and art dealers who've been ripped off to the tune of two million dollars by some of the cleverest art forgeries to come on the market in decades.'

'Forgeries? You mean like faking Old Masters, that sort of thing?'

'Uh-huh.'

'And Sefton was doing the forgeries?'

'Not Sefton. Leon. He did the actual fakin'. Sefton looked after the disposal. He set up the whole operation. 'Tween them they had a nice little racket goin'.'

'Are you certain?'

'I sure as hell would be if I'd got a look at the contents of Owls Watch before it went up in smoke. There *had* to be some hard evidence lying around.'

'I think there was,' Goddard offered, remembering all the material in the little annexe studio. He told Medwin about it, trying to recall everything he'd seen there. Medwin raised his eyebrows and kept giving low little whistles as Goddard itemised the camera equipment, the old canvases and frames, the Madonna illustrations in the art books, the strange looking jars and brushes and paint knives, everything.

'It figures,' Medwin nodded, standing up and beginning to pace back and forward. 'Most of these bunko merchants – you know, guys like Sefton and Leon – most of them usually pass the forgeries off as the work of an "artist unknown". Maybe some old monk, or a promising young artist who died before reachin' his prime. They steer clear of the big names like Da Vinci or Rembrandt. Too risky. Their usual *modus operandi* is to offer the fake as a newly discovered work by some reasonably well-known artist. It's passed off as belongin' to the artist's "obscure" period, say when he was only experimentin' with different techniques, or to some period in the artist's life that isn't too well documented. Like, for instance, when he may have lived quietly in some foreign city or remote mountain village.'

'Or some obscure little island off the Irish coast?'

'Exactly.'

'But how would the faker know that?'

'Easy. If you were to buy a few good books on some of these old Dutch or Italian painters you'd find that there's a helluva lot of blanks in their lives. Lots of "transitional" periods. Gaps. That, kid, is where the faker strikes. He concentrates on the gaps, the transitional periods. Then he comes up with a canvas that might very well have been painted in just such a period.'

'What about the art experts, wouldn't they detect it straight off?'

'Not if the faker knows the game inside out and almost as well as the so-called experts. In fact guys like Leon are the *real* experts. F'rinstance they'd use a support stripped from a paintin' that wasn't worth more than a few bucks, the kinda nickle and dime stuff picked up around the junk shops. But the thing is they'd make sure that the support dated from the period or the locality of the planned forgery. Also, they'd use obsolete pigments and varnish. They'd be familiar with such data as which artist used linseed or walnut oil —'

'Walnut? Leon had little jars with labels like walnut oil and bone white and something called, I think, cera colla. Stuff like that.'

'*Jeez*! See what I mean? Leon obviously knew the game

every damn bit as good as the experts.'

'What's so special about walnut oil?' Goddard was now carefully polishing his black shoes.

'Nuthin' really. 'Course it's been round since the Middle Ages but it's never been as popular as linseed oil. Da Vinci valued it. And some of the other masters used it and recommended its use with certain pigments. It becomes rancid with age. By such little things the experts can tell a lot. Little things like which oil, which pigments, what kinda brush, how the strokes were laid on, pentimento —'

'*Penti*-what?'

'Pentimento. Italian word. It's when the artist "repents" his original design and paints over it again. It's a kinda reappearance of part of the original design on the finished oil paintin'. It results in an increasin' transparency of the overpaintin' as it ages.'

'You seem to know a lot about art.'

'That's what they pay me for,' Medwin shrugged.

'Yeah, but I still don't follow this "pentimento" thing.'

'Okay. Say f'rinstance a checkerboard marble floor was painted by the artist before the figures and furniture were put in on the canvas. So, maybe the black squares of the floor would eventually show through the lighter colours of, say, a woman's gown in the foreground. Get it? That's what the art experts mean by pentimento. And, often, that's how they can date or authenticate a genuine paintin'.'

'I see.' Goddard's interest was growing. 'What happens if the forger can't get his hands on old material, if he has to use modern oils and stuff?'

'No problem. He just "ages" the work.'

'How?'

'Lots of ways. One method is to buy up antique canvases and then paint over them with modern oils. But first the faker gotta squeeze the oils from the tube onto a sheet of ordinary blottin' paper. He leaves them for a day or two so that the blotter soaks up most of the oil and the impurities. Then, by usin' zinc white and egg tempera as a medium he mixes the colours from the blotter and goes to work. When the finished paintin' is dry he gives it a layer of size and holds it in front of an electric fire. As the size dries out and contracts the paintin' will crack. Hey presto, it's aged! Then all it needs is to be "dug up".'

'Dug up?'

'Well if they don't have any documentation to corroborate the work they usually have a sophisticated scheme whereby it's accidentally "dug up" in the cellar of some Italian villa or some old attic in Paris.'

'What about modern scientific detection?' Goddard was now carefully combing his hair and examining his reflection in the mirror. 'Don't the art galleries and the experts use X-Ray or ultra-violet light to find out if it's genuine?'

'Sure. X-Ray, gamma-ray shadowgraph, infra-red, standard chemical analyses, dating of organic materials by measuring the residual radioactivity of carbon. Yeah, they've got all that shit. But by the time it's called in to put a check on the paintin' in question the merchandise has usually changed hands and the bogus art dealer has disappeared. Also, in the States your average fat cat millionaire on a culture high, or lookin' for a good investment, ain't likely to realise he's bought a fake until years later when the dumb bastard tries to sell it.' Medwin had ceased his pacing and was now gazing into the mirror, addressing Goddard's reflection. 'You see, kid, for most artists there's generally only a small proportion of works whose history is completely known and documented. And very few that can be definitely traced back to a sale by the artist himself. All the rest — the vast bulk of paintin's on the international market — come under a different headin'. A more dubious headin'. Take that with the fact that over the past thirty years there's been some mighty big money paid out for old paintin's and you can see how a good faker can hit the jackpot. A really good faker, that is. A guy like Leon.'

'The jackpot certainly hit him today,' Goddard said, moving away from the mirror. 'Tell me more about the art swindling racket.'

'Yeah, well, like I was sayin', there's always the danger of bein' caught off base if the faker tries to imitate one of the big names, Titian or Raphael or Rembrandt, say. But if he sticks to an artist, or artists, on whom there's no work catalogue and no reputable scholarly data, then the faker is on much safer ground. And onto big money.'

Medwin was warming to his theme. 'In a way, I guess, the art market is really to blame for the fakers. It needs the goods. The new rich and the culture craze and the collectin' boom and all that jazz means that the art dealers gotta keep supplyin' the market. And there's always someone somewhere who can somehow dispose of almost anythin'. Add to that the fact that the art world sets great store on the confidentiality of transactions. They like to protect the clients' names from the public. So it becomes a whole grey area in which the faker thrives.'

'But surely the dealers have to protect their own reputations as well?'

'Yeah, but they also reckon that their reputation will be damaged if they have to admit that they handled a forgery, knowingly or unknowingly. So, if they find that someone's unloaded a dud on them they usually get rid of it at some out-of-town auction or pass it down market for some less reputable dealer to dispose of.'

Medwin sat down on the bed again. 'Say, do you have a drink hereabouts? All this talkin' ....'

'No, sorry. But let's go down to the bar. I'm very interested in what you're saying.'

'Sure thing.' Medwin was up with alacrity.

'Only *one* drink, mind you. I've got a dinner date.'

'The blonde? Can't say I blame you.'

'One drink. You know how it is. Two is company ....'

'Three is a crowd. Yeah, I get the picture.'

Goddard followed him out of the room, jabbing the light switch by the door and plunging everything into the darkness — except the corridor.

And the brunette.

She was just a few feet from the door to Goddard's room, very busily putting a few finishing flicks to her hair with the aid of a comb and one of the corridor's mirrors. She didn't look at them. But Goddard certainly looked at her. It was impossible not to. Without the heavy glasses and the tweed skirt — she was dressed for dinner, he guessed, in a bright red blouse and black skirt, the suggestion of something like pearls, or a necklace, or a gold chain drawing immediate attention to her delicate neck and the fine bone structure of her face and the large, dark, luminous eyes that peered intently at their own beautiful reflection — and now, without the scholarly trimmings, she was a strikingly attractive young woman. If, by any chance, Miss Gloria Fontana were to stand him up, then perhaps ....?

'Good evening.' He wanted to linger.

'Oh, eh ... good evening.' She didn't move her eyes from the mirror.

As they went down the corridor Medwin whispered: 'Think she was lissenin' in on us?'

Goddard, suddenly uncertain, muttered: 'You're the private eye. You tell me.'

'Beautiful dames like her don't usually travel alone. Also, they usually do their tittivatin' and glamour work in their own rooms before, not in a goddam public corridor.' Medwin glanced back over his shoulder. 'I think we're gonna havta check this one out. What d'ya say?'

'What do you mean "we", paleface? Christ, I've enough problems! I need a drink.'

At the bar, and over the first whiskey, they continued their earlier conversation. Goddard said: 'You were telling me about art forgeries and reputable dealers. What about art historians and scholars? Wouldn't they recognise a fake?'

'With most of them it's the same thing. If they intentionally or otherwise give a wrong attribution on a paintin' they're not likely to advertise the fact, are they? And once the experts — the historians and scholars — accept a forgery as genuine, well then the faker is home and dried.'

'How?'

''Cause all his other fakes from the same stable will be judged authentic by comparin' them with the first one. Get it? The forger is on to a goldmine. Guys like Leon and Sefton are cleanin' up!'

'What put you onto Sefton?'

'Well, to start with he was only a small piece in a big jig-saw. A very small piece. The big pieces were the number of high-priced forgeries suddenly croppin' up all over the place — New York, Philly, Chicago, the West Coast. A lotta rich guys found they'd been taken for a ride. And so a lot of the big galleries and the most important dealers got together and decided something had to be done. That's when the Benwood Agency was called in. At first we'd little to go on. Only that the fakes were originatin' in Europe. Like I said, most of them were "dug up" in old Italian villages, Bavarian beer cellars, London junk shops. That sort of thing. Most of them came in through the legitimate art world. A few were smuggled in. We had to check out every lead, every story, every goddam paintin'. Mostly it's slow, tedious, routine work. Also you gotta have a helluva lotta contacts. In my case I liaise with a few buddies in US Customs, NYPD, the narcotic squad. So, about four years back one of these guys was doin' a routine check on some machine parts that had just been unloaded on Pier Twenny-six, some farm machinery imported from Europe. Probably on the look-out for drugs. Anyway, in one piece of equipment he found a rolled-up canvas hidden inside a hollow tube of metal. Turned out to be another one of the fakes. Venetian school, as I recall. Good too.'

'Get to the point. What about Sefton?'

'Nudder thing about my line of business is that you gotta learn patience. Remember that Joe. Patience.'

'Okay, so I'm patiently waiting to hear how you tied Sefton into this international smuggling or swindling or whatever.'

'An' I'm gonna tellya soon as ya stop interruptin', 'Chrissake!'

'Sorry.'

'So, naturally we had to run a check on anyone who had access to the particular mechanical equipment. 'Course anyone could have put the rolled-up canvas in there — one of the ship's crew, a longshoreman this side of the Atlantic, factory worker, truck driver — just about anyone.'

'Sefton, what about *him*?'

'Sefton happens to be the marketin' manager with the company exportin' the machinery. As such he was naturally part of our routine check. Routine, nothin' more. He was interviewed along with about two dozen other guys. Very co-operative. We'd no reason to suspect him any more than half a dozen other guys.'

'So?'

65

'So have you seen his place here on this goddam sod of turf they call an island?'

'No.'

'I have. Only from the outside, I admit. Since I got here a few days back I've been doin' a quiet bit of snoopin'. Sefton's place is about a mile beyond Owls Watch, beside some old monastic ruin. Very classy joint. At least fifteen rooms I'd guess. Outdoor heated pool, tennis court, stables, the works.'

'That doesn't mean anything.'

'By itself, no. But like I said, I liaise with a lotta old buddies. Internal Revenue, State Department, Commerce, FBI, you name it. I do them a favour, they do me a favour. What do I learn? I learn that our friend Sefton has a similar set-up in the Bahamas, 'nudder in the south of France, with a yacht thrown in, a shootin' lodge in Scotland and high-class apartments in London, Paris, Rome and Munich.'

'So what? You've just said that he owns a big exporting business.'

'I didn't say it was *that* big. An' I didn't say he owns it. Point of fact, kid, it's not such a big outfit and he's *only* the international marketin' manager. He doesn't even hold any stock worth talkin' about. Only a salaried manager. No big deal. So how come he can afford this lifestyle?'

'Maybe he married money,' Goddard offered.

Medwin smiled and shook his head: 'The first Mrs Sefton is a lush who he divorced and to whom he has to hand out a sizeable chunk in alimony and sanatoria charges. The present Mrs Sefton, whatever else she has goin' for her, it ain't money. She's a good looker I grant ya, and before Sefton met her she was a part-time model who did a bit of high-class hookin' for her bread. But she's not money, Joe. No way. We ran a thorough check on her. No, that's not where the money comes from.'

'Where then?'

'Okay, let's put a few things together an' see if they don't add up. First, Sefton has property here and there an' a life style that certainly can't be accounted for by his only known means of income. Right?'

'Right.' Goddard caught Mammy's eye and indicated the two near-empty whiskey glasses with a little "same again" gesture.

'Second, he spends a few months here on the island every year, living close by, and on fairly intimate terms with, the artist Arthur Leon. Right?' Medwin had started with his thumb, then the forefinger and was now about to tick off the second finger. 'Third, on the floor above his apartment in Rome an artist named Natale Di Como used to have his studio. Di Como is known to have dabbled in copying the Old Masters. He's also known to have played golf with Sefton in the mornings and to have played a different kinda ball game with Mrs Sefton in the evenings.' Medwin moved onto the next finger: 'When Sefton wasn't using his villa in the south of France he rented it out to an artist named Norbert Du Fey. Du Fey first made a name for himself by his excellent copying of the Impressionists twenty years back. He keeps a rather low profile nowadays, ever since he was implicated in some homosexual scandal back in the 70s.' He was now down to the little finger. 'In London our Mr Sefton belongs to a club, one of whose members was Algernon Mickleburgh. Ever heard of Mickleburgh?'

'No.'

'I didn't think so. But Mickleburgh, who painted in the style of Constable and who was a dab hand at Turner-like landscapes, frequently played backgammon with our Mr Sefton and has been photographed in the society and gossip pages as an escort for Miss Karen Sefton whenever that young lady cared to go night clubbing and disco dancing. Want to hear more?'

'Shoot.'

'Shoot. I like it. Very apt Joe. Because a frequent visitor to Sefton's hunting lodge in the Highlands was an old picture restorer named Tom Archibold. Archibold is a whiskey alcoholic but when he's working he has a steady hand. Apart from grouse shooting and salmon fishing and other such outdoor activities with the Seftons Archibold is reckoned to be an authority on all those Victorian and Landseer and sporting prints. Are you getting the picture?'

'More or less.'

'Good. Sefton's Paris pad is slap bang up beside the studio of a junky called Emile Boulanger. In his more lucid moments Boulanger has been described as another Van Gogh. They say that any day now he's going to lop off his ear. Either that or his pecker, because they also say that he's growing tired of Mrs Sefton's interest in it. Next, in Munich, and just round the corner from the Sefton apartment, there lives a gifted young painter named Dieter Krefeld who has a good eye for Cubism, Post-Impressionism, Karen Sefton-ism and ....'

'Okay,' Goddard conceded just as Medwin was running out of fingers. 'What you're saying is that Sefton, perhaps using his women as decoys, cultivates the acquaintance of a certain type of artist and then gets the artist to turn his skills to forgery. Am I right?'

'Go to the top of the class Joe. That's it in a nutshell.'

'But can you *prove* it?'

'Like I said, if I'd gotten into Leon's place for a look around I'm certain I'd have come away with all the proof I need.'

'None of this tells us anything about who killed Leon.'

'Not yet. But what I've told you just now, and when I give it to the local cops, it's gotta take a lot of the heat off you.'

'I certainly hope so.'

'Sure it has. Leon's murder *has* to be tied into the whole business. The art forgeries. Sefton. The lot. Someone — I don't know who — was into a double cross.'

'That's what doesn't make sense Hank. Today, witnessing that little scene when the Seftons drove up to the burning cottage, I was ready to lay money on the jealousy angle. Either one of the women, or Sefton when he realised that Leon was playing around with both of them. But that hardly makes sense in the case of a man who was using his wife and his daughter as bait. He must have anticipated the risk.'

'Maybe he had too much trust in the bait. Sometimes the fisherman doesn't intend the bait to be swallowed.'

'Stick to detective work Hank. I don't trust you on fishing.' Fly-fishing from the shore! Medwin wasn't all that smart after all. Especially when Goddard began to ponder some of the other questions. 'There's another thing — even if you had discovered all the necessary proof that Leon was faking pictures that still doesn't mean you could link it to Sefton, does it?'

'Depends on what I might've found,' he shrugged. 'But what I *can* link to him is this: over the past five-six years, in every one of the major US cities in which one of these art swindles was perpetrated, Sefton visited each of those cities in the week before the swindle. We have it on record.'

'How?'

'Easy. Airline records. Hotels. Computer checks. You know kid, you can get a lot of data from those newfangled slot machines. Okay, so ostensibly Sefton was there on legit business trips. But you have to admit that's pretty solid stuff when taken in conjunction with what I just told you about all his next door neighbours in Europe being painters with a reputation for art imitation.'

'That's something else, why don't you nose around for the necessary evidence in their studios? Maybe you'll find what you were looking for at Owls Watch.'

'That's just it Joe,' Medwin sighed, then quickly downed what was left of his drink. 'This is where I hit the "tough shit" stage of the scenario. All those other guys — Di Como in Rome, Du Fey in Cannes, Mickleburgh in London, Archibold in Scotland, Boulanger in Paris, Krefeld in Munich — all those guys, over the past two years, have either disappeared, are in jail, or dead. Their studios are dismantled and closed down. The trail is cold.'

'I take it then that Leon was your last shot?'

'Yeah, 'specially while the Seftons were vacationin' here at the same time. All the eggs in one basket, so to speak. Also, 'cause of its seclusion, Owls Watch should've been easier to break inta than any of those big city joints on the continent.' He sighed again. 'That fire today sure fucked up all the evidence.'

'Maybe not,' Goddard swished the last of his whiskey and ice. 'Maybe my pictures might throw up something.'

'Think so?'

'I hope so. Remember, I seem to be suspect number one in a murder case.'

'I'll help you beat the rap.' Medwin punched his arm lightly, enthusiastically. 'We work together on this, okay?'

'Okay.'

'We have a deal Joe?'

'We have a deal.'

'My friends call me Hank —'

'We have a deal Hank.'

Why not, Goddard thought. For a start he needed everyone and anything that might help to prove his innocence in the matter of Arthur Leon's death. And secondly, his professional instinct told him that he was onto the biggest scoop of his career. Probably the scoop of the decade!

'See ya round Joe,' Medwin smiling, winking, flopped off the tall bar stool. 'Here comes your dinner date. By the way, don't tell her too much just yet, okay?'

'Okay Hank.'

Gloria — gorgeous in a little black off-the-shoulder number — entered and came towards him. Smiling ....

5

The diningroom was all dark panelling below, exposed brickwork above, and with a mock-Tudor ceiling from the blackened beams of which a few wispy plants and ferns, in open baskets, trailed downwards. It was a ten-table room, four high-backed chairs to a table, and each table had a bottled candle set squarely in the centre of a red tablecloth. The colour of the tablecloths matched the drapes, which were drawn tightly across the bay window embrazure, trying to shut out the storm and the black rivers of rain disfiguring the panes. Even with the windows securely fastened the heavy drapes kept swaying fitfully and in time to the rattling panes. But there was nothing cold or draughty about the dining room. The massive fireplace crackled with burning logs and shimmered with the glowing whitish-orange of peat sods. Over the mantel-piece was a gold-trimmed mirror that threw back the warm, mellow light of the room.

Goddard would have liked to photograph her in this light, in soft focus, her face perfect in candle glow, the background dusty gold and faintly blurred. Her eyes were bluey-green, depthless, with curious lights of humour and sensitivity and cool assessment — and perhaps just the tiniest echoes of tiredness and the strain from the day's events. She was beautiful.

So too was the brunette. For a little while just now she had been the only other occupant of the room, picking slowly at her fish salad with a paperback novel propped against a water jug before her. When Goddard and Gloria first entered, after a half-hour of aperitifs in the bar, Medwin, finishing his ice cream dessert, had waved to them. After coffee he'd departed hurriedly, pausing for just a few moments at their table to bid *bon appetit*, and then waddling off either towards the bar or his room. A little while later the brunette left.

Goddard, relishing the sense of 'aloneness' and near intimacy, reached for the half-empty wine bottle and tippled it into both glasses. 'Here's looking at you kid — or should I say Gloria?'

'Gloria's fine. Cheers Joe.' They touched glasses. 'Actually my name isn't Gloria. Not really. That's sort of a stage name. I'm a dancer, you see. My real name — the one I was born with — is Maggie Black. Here, what's so funny?'

'Nothing.'

'Don't laugh then. Actually my agent made me change it to Gloria Fontana. Said it would look better in lights.'

'And does it?'

'Not lately. It did once or twice back some years ago. Then, when I married, it changed to Mrs Arthur Leon.'

He suddenly realised that she was not the hard-bitten tough little woman-of-the-world that she tried so hard to be. The brittle mid-Atlantic accent had slipped somewhat and a kind of working-class Cockney echo was edging through. And he guessed that underneath all the brashness there was a lonely, scared little kid.

Scared, or guilty?

'Tell me about Leon.'

'Not much to tell about a bloke like Arty. He was a rat, plain and simple.'

'How did you meet him?'

'I was working in a West End club at the time. I was just gone seventeen and I'd landed my first job in a chorus line. It was a nice, well-run place and I loved the work. Arty came in one night with some other students from the Slade. He was studying to be a painter. After the show we got talking. In those days he was a real handsome fella. Very pleasant, very charming, very witty. Anyway, like I said, I was only seventeen and I thought he was the greatest thing since the sliced pan.'

'So you fell in love with him?'

'Yeah. Well, at the time I *thought* it was love. You know, the real thing. Like in a novel or in the movies. I was very young, remember. Anyway, we started going out together and after a few weeks we got married. Soon after that everything started to change.'

'In what way?'

'Well, Arty wanted to be a painter even more than I wanted to be a dancer. Which meant he had to do an awful lot of studying. And which meant that I had to earn the rent. And Arty wasn't the sort to settle for anything less than a fairly posh Chelsea place complete with rooftop studio. Not that I minded in the early days. Like I said, I was young and starry-eyed. Still, it meant I had to hold down two jobs. Waitress by day, dancer by night.'

'Didn't Arty try his hand at any kind of work at all?'

Gloria shook her head: 'Said menial stuff had a bad effect on his inspiration. And oh boy, did that guy have inspiration! I'll say he did!'

'Was he that good?'

'As a painter, I think so. But I was referring to how inspired he was at finding work for me. He made me quit the club and work in a different place. Not nearly so posh, but it paid more 'cause the hours were longer. After that a different club, then another. All the time earning more, working harder and drifting down the scale into sleazier joints. Finally I was working a fifteen hour stint, three separate shifts, four separate strip joints.'

She took a long drink from her glass before resuming: 'I didn't like the work but I didn't complain too much 'cause I thought I was helping his career. Around that time he was beginning to sell a few of his paintings and making a name for himself. Also, though I didn't know it at the time, he was making it with a few of those rich society females. I should've suspected something 'cause he was always out when I got home. And he was spending an awful lot of money. We were always in debt.' She turned the big grey eyes on him: 'You see Joe, I was still only a kid and I had this romantic notion of share and share alike. Only I was the one doing the sharing. I gave Arty my pay packet every week. Okay, I know it was stupid, but I really thought the bastard was banking it for both of us. You know, rainy day stuff. Or maybe a deposit on a nice little house where someday we could bring up a few kids and be a *real* family. But the bills kept coming in. Eventually they'd mounted so high that the only way to meet them was for me to ....' She paused, fingered her glass in silence for a few moments, and then tossed back the drink in one gulp.

'Arty knew an awful lot of weirdo people. He fixed it up with some chap that I, eh — well, that I should pose for some pictures. They were fairly tatty. You know, sort of pornographic stuff.' She refilled her glass. 'I'm not proud of what I did Joe, but I still had some feeling left for Arty and I thought once we got out from under the debts we still had a chance to make a go of our marriage. I only posed for that stuff once. That's all. And I felt dirty. Cheap. Used. So when he asked me to do the same again a week later I refused. And that's when I had my first real dust-up with Arty. He got very rough. I was the only stripper that night who had to cake the make-up over the bruises — ribs, thighs, arms and face.'

Goddard's angry grimace was genuine.

'Thanks Joe.' She reached out with an appreciative hand and briefly touched his. 'After that the fights became more frequent. Real ding-dong stuff. 'Specially when I found out about the other dolly birds. 'Course he didn't need me then. He was in with all the jet set crowd and flashing around the West End with some rich bitch of a debutante. The final bust-up came when he had the gall to try ditching me with the suggestion that he'd recommend me to an important mate of his who ran a fairly high-class call girl agency. Very high-class, and naturally good old Arty would be onto a percentage. That did it. I threw a plate of spaghetti at him. We were shouting and screaming and wrecking the kitchen and when he told me to go to hell I told him I'd already been there thanks to him, and when he let fly with his fist I belted him over the head with a wine bottle and while he was staggering and bending over the sink and mopping blood off his forehead and his eighty quid silk shirt I just stormed out of the place.'

'Did he follow you?'

'I don't know. And I didn't care. That night I stayed with a girl-friend of mine who'd been with me in the chorus line at the first club I'd worked. She was with a troupe going out to the States in a couple of days and as they were stuck for a last-minute replacement she fixed it so that I got the job.'

'What about Leon, did you ever see him again?'

'Not until today. I stayed out in America for a few years. A hoofer, most of the time. Las Vegas, Miami, Broadway once or twice. It wasn't such a bad life. Now and again I'd see bits in the papers about Arty. Mostly the gossip columns. He was becoming a big name round London in cafe society and artistic circles. But we'd no contact. Not a phone call, not a letter. Nothing. Not even when I filed for divorce. That was all done through the lawyers. No contact, until ....' She paused.

'Until ...?' he coaxed.

'No contact until last month.'

'How did that come about?'

'I came home from the States a few years back with another dance outfit. We called ourselves 'Checkerboard'. Three black girls, three white girls, costumes to match. Maybe you've seen us on TV?'

Goddard shook his head: 'I'm certain I would've remembered you.'

'We do mostly variety, summer show stuff, the clubs. We've been doing okay 'cause we've got a good agent. Anyway, about three months ago Bernie — that's the agent — got me to audition for the lead part in a new musical. Big West End production. I can sing a bit as well as dance and I'd already taken drama classes in the States, but I didn't really think I'd get anywhere. So you can imagine how it was when Bernie rang me one day and told me that both the producer and the leading man wanted me for the part. I was over the moon! Even before we went into rehearsal Bernie had signed up everything and he was putting out all the publicity razz-ma-tazz — you know, my picture in all the show magazines, the tabloids, TV chat shows. Suddenly I'm an overnight success. Maybe you saw some of those newspaper pictures of me?'

'Maybe, but I'm sure I would've remembered.'

'Anyway, *someone* certainly saw them. Arty. And he remembered. Next thing I knew he was on the phone to Bernie. Same old Arty, full of smarmy congratulations and all that shit. Then came the clincher. He'd still held onto the negatives of those porno pictures from way back and he wanted to know what it was worth to me or Bernie not to release them to the gutter press.'

'But that's blackmail! Why didn't you go to the police?'

Gloria shook her head: 'That's what I said, but Bernie and the producer were afraid of any bad publicity for the show. In fact the producer was all for buying back my contract and pulling me out of the show, but Bernie finally talked him round into giving me the chance to come here and to try and buy the pictures back from Arty.'

'I see. And that explains what we were searching for at Owls Watch — or rather, what *you* were searching for ....'

'I'm not so sure I like the way you put that Joe.' She tried to smile as she raised the glass. Goddard envied the brief gleam of red wine on her lips. 'You don't think I killed Arty, do you?'

'What the hell,' he said, a bit tipsy now, waving his hand expansively. 'The kinky photos have gone up in smoke along with everything else.'

'Yeah, only now I'm a suspect in a murder case. How about that for bad publicity?' There was a hint of a wry smile about the lips as she suddenly pushed back her chair and stood up.

'Hey, hold on a minute — what's the hurry?'

'Goodnight Joe.'

'Gloria, hang on awhile — how about a night cap?'

'Thanks, but it's been a rough day. I think I'll turn in.'

As he was rising, struggling from his chair, she came quickly round the table and sketched a perfunctory butterfly kiss on his cheek. 'Goodnight, Joe. Thanks for everything.'

'Gloria ....?'

And just as quickly she was gone.

Goddard didn't feel like finishing what little was left of the wine. He just sat there staring at the guttering flame of the bottled candle. After a few minutes Murty — still in his waiter's garb — detached himself from the shadows and began to prepare the other tables for tomorrow's breakfast.

'Would sir care for a teenie night cap before retiring?'

'What? ... No thanks, Murty. Sir has had a rough day. In fact sir is fucked and he thinks he'll turn in ....'

'As you wish, Mr Goddard. Goodnight.'

"Night ....'

But two hours later Goddard was still slowly and reflectively pacing his room. Earlier, spread-eagled on the bed and assailed by the wailing sounds of the storm outside, he'd tried to snatch at sleep. It, like the solution to so many of the questions that hounded him, was elusive. Now, clad only in his vest and underpants, he paced back and forth pondering the day's events. Maybe he should have taken that night cap after all. Was it too late to ring down for room service?

The storm noises almost drowned out the faint, but insistent, *rat-tat-tatting* on his door. When he eventually became aware of it he called: 'Who's there? Hold on a minute!' as he struggled back into his trousers. 'Who is it?'

'Me. Gloria.' A loud whisper through the wooden panel. 'Hey, Joe ...?'

'Just a minute.' When he'd checked his fly buttons he opened the door.

Aimed right at his navel was a small wooden tray holding a half bottle of gin, ice, mixers and two glasses. Gloria was behind it, coming out of the shadows, beautiful and nocturnal and slinky in a silky dressing gown and her hair out of the ponytail and falling carelessly and luxuriantly to her shoulders. A deliciously intoxicating fragrance wafted in with her as she glided into his room with the tray. 'Shut the door, Joe.'

'Sure, but —?'

'I can't sleep. Joe, do you have a bottle opener or a toothbrush or a comb or any damn thing that gives me an excuse to stay awhile and talk?'

She placed the tray on the counterpane and sat down beside it, answering his look in a small, almost scared, voice: 'Joe, this place gives me the willies. I think it's all that silence out there.'

'On a point of fact Gloria, there happens to be a howling gale outside.'

'That's what I mean,' she nodded, her shoulders moving in a kind of involuntary shudder as she began to pour from the gin bottle. 'It's scary. Don't you miss the sound of traffic? Taxies, buses, cars?'

'Not really.'

'I do, Joe. And I can't sleep. And I want to stay awhile, d'you mind? And I want you to talk to me, okay?'

'Okay, but what do you want to talk about?'

She was silent for just long enough to add the ice and mixer. Then she looked up suddenly and asked: 'Joe, you don't think *I* killed Arty, do you?'

'Of course not,' he shrugged the lie and the uncertainty off as he reached for a proferred glass.

'I know it looks bad. I mean, I *did* have a motive ....'

'Nonsense!'

'I often felt like killing the creep in the past. But a quick blast from a shotgun wouldn't have been my method. The bastard deserved something slow and painful and long drawn out.'

'Please, Gloria. Respect for the dead.' Goddard took a sip and then sat down beside her.

'Yeah, you're right Joe. I didn't really mean that —

though he was a real rat, was Arty. He really fouled up a lot of my life. That's why I felt so scary and spooky in my own room. Wouldn't surprise me if he came back to haunt me just for the hell of it.'

'He's dead Gloria. Finito.'

'Yeah, and I wish I knew who did it.'

'Hope you don't think it was me.'

"Course not. I was right behind you on the road to Owls Watch. All the way. I saw you ringing at the front door and then going round the back of the house. I was only a few minutes behind you. I would've heard the shots.'

'That's something I've been meaning to ask you Gloria. You left the hotel about twenty minutes before I did, right?'

'Right, but I took Murty's directions up the wrong way. I always had a lousy sense of direction. When I got to the top of the main street I turned right instead of left. I went on for about a mile and then I met some farmer bloke and I checked with him for Owls Watch. He put me right and so I had to double back. That's when I saw you up ahead, though I'd no idea that you were heading for Owls Watch as well.'

So that explained the time lapse! It explained everything. Goddard was so relieved that he could have hugged her. He did, in a way. While she'd been talking Gloria had shivered once or twice — whether from remembrance of finding the dead body or from the cold, he couldn't tell — but Goddard pulled the counterpane up about her shoulders and held it there with his hand resting lightly on her arm. Now he just tightened his hold and drew her a bit closer to him.

'Look, I know what you're thinking Joe. But it's not like that. Honest. It's just that this place gives me the creeps. It's ever so spooky ....'

Something about the set of her features — the shape

of her face, oval, tapering into a sensitive mouth and chin, the eyes wide and grey and lovely and with tiny little glints of uncertainty or fear in them — something got to him there and then.

'I just want to talk ... need company ....'

'I could tell you to piss off,' he grinned.

'But you won't, will you?'

'No.'

'You're sweet, Joe, d'you know that?' Her face came round to meet his, smiling a little. Then she kissed him. The lips, this time. She was about to pull away after a few moments, but he tightened his hold on her with one hand, using the other to leave down his glass and to remove the glass from her hand. It was a long, slow, lingering kiss ....

... A long time afterwards — lying together under the sheets, Gloria's warm, soft, naked body pressed close to his, and her fingers dancing gently across his bare chest — she whispered into his ear: 'Know how I *really* know you couldn't have killed Arty?'

'No. How?'

'Whoever killed Arty—just blasting him away at close quarters like that — well, whoever did that had no subtlety. No finesse. Some men are like that when it comes to making love. Wham, slam, bam, thank you ma'am. But you're not the wham-slam type, Joe. You're gentle and slow and subtle and considerate and ....'

'That's because I always use two different techniques. One for murder. The other for nookey.'

'Liar.'

He pressed her closer to him and asked: 'Do you still find the silence spooky?'

'Not any more. I like the way you have of raising the noise level. Like to make some more noise Joe?'

Maybe it was in that moment he realised that he was

falling for the beautiful Gloria Fontana and the hard-bitten Widow Leon and the scared kid Maggie Black. All three of her.

6

He woke suddenly, not sure of what had woken him. There was a depressing emptiness about his bed, a kind of deserted feeling. A lack of warmth. Perfume. Presence. The same emptiness pervaded the room. Where was Gloria?

He fumbled for the bedside lamp. His watch told him that it was 4.38. It couldn't tell him what had woken him. There was no noise. Maybe that was it — the silence? Some time during the past few hours the storm had worn itself out. The screeching winds and the torrents of rain were now only the faintest sigh, the half-heard whisper of drizzling rain, the merest echo of the furious downpour that had been raging ever since the lot of them had raced away from the burning cottage and down to —

Wait a minute! If it had been pelting rain all that time — nine, ten hours at least — maybe the rain had put out the fire ages ago? It was possible, wasn't it? And if so then maybe the fire hadn't destroyed everything. The murder weapon, clues, letters, the photos that might incriminate Gloria — anything could be lying out there under a layer of rain-sodden ashes. And by daylight there would be a lot of nosy-parkers sifting through the debris.

He got out of bed and dressed quickly. He thought about going to Gloria's room and telling her what he had in mind. Then he decided against it. If he was to show some initiative and single-handedly search out and find the photos before the police and then hand them over to Gloria — without peeking at them? — or maybe destroy them, then she'd be both impressed and eternally grateful. More important, perhaps, he might just happen on something that might help to shift the suspicion away from Gloria and himself. It was worth a try!

He pulled on his slacks and a sweater. His anorak was still a bit damp but into the pockets he shoved cigarettes, matches, pencil flash-lamp and, out of habit, the 35mm Nikon. Then he slipped quietly from the room.

There was a night light at the end of the corridor and another small table lamp on the reception desk. Everywhere else was dark and shadowy but he had enough visibility to navigate to the front door and he managed it safely across the parquet flooring on tip-toe. He eased the bolt off the door and stepped outside. The main street of the village — the entire island it seemed — was in total darkness. No street lamps, no house lights, not a single person up and about, and no sound save the steady plip-plop of rain from a gutter and the gentle soughing of the sea breeze. And it was like that all the way out the road to Owls Watch, out past Jack Sweeney's unlit bungalow and the other scattered, shadowy houses

By the time he reached the burnt-out shell of Leon's cottage the seething blackness was just beginning to give way to a lesser darkness — not light, but a grey murkiness seeping in from the east. This time he was able to go in through the front door. Or rather, what was left of it — a few bits of damp, still-warm, charred laths that powdered into black ash wherever his boots touched them. There was a dank, smoky, acrid smell everywhere.

And an eerie feeling. Especially when he thought about the blackened skeleton lying close by under the smouldering rubble. That was the very last place he wanted to search.

After a few moments of casting about indecisively with the aid of his little flash-lamp he located a longish piece of metal rod — a piece of blackened aluminium piping or something like that — and with it he began to poke through the debris, turning over steamy little mounds of still-smouldering ashes and scattering them about. He concentrated his search on what remained of the other rooms and what had been the little photographic studio, taking care to avoid the area where he estimated the charred skeleton might be. He spent an hour like this, raking and sifting and scattering ashes and turning things over with his toecap. Nothing. He'd been wrong about the rain. The fire had swept through the entire house, gutting everything.

Or almost everything. In a tiny porch leading out onto the garden he made a partial discovery. Some roof tiles and plasterboard had fallen through onto the stone floor, sandwiching some old magazines, a few newspapers and what appeared to be a couple of discarded sketch-pads. They had been partially protected from the fire until the rain had come to their rescue. Goddard carefully fished out the sketch pads and examined them under the ray of his pocket lamp. The edges of the sheets, and some of the topmost leaves, were charred and brittle and sodden, and they smudged and crumpled and fell apart almost as soon as he touched them. But the centres of the pages were dry and intact. He took them outside into the garden and laid them out on the damp surface of a stone garden seat. It was difficult to peel back the pages without further damage but he tried, gingerly, slowly.

They were all pencil or pen-and-ink sketches. A few

landscapes, but mostly nude studies. Almost pornographic, Goddard considered. They were certainly erotic, sexy doodles, the breasts highlighted and pushed out, the legs angled enticingly, the facial features of the models much less pronounced than the shading of the nipples or the delicate smudges of pubic hair. And Goddard had to admit that Leon had certainly been a damn fine artist. Every one of the sketches was a little work of art. And though the breasts, thighs and pubic shading were very much to the fore in the compositions — the facial details were seldom more than the briefest of deft lines — it was still possible to discern who the models had been.

One of the sketch books was made up of naughty, pop art and hoydenish studies of the youthful Karen Sefton. There was no mistaking her. There she was in every one of the expert scribbles and doodles — naked, except for her riding boots and little bowler hat, her distinctive ponytail hair dangling over one shoulder, the black riding crop variously clutched, caressed, held or brandished as a phallic symbol. She pouted and smiled and ogled from every charred page in the most provocative pose and stance.

It was much the same with the second sketch pad, all of the step-mother, Mrs Sefton. Every charred or sodden page was devoted to the same sort of titillating studies — a more mature nakedness to be sure, more classical, odalisque postures, but there could be no mistaking the dark-haired beauty and the full-bodied attractiveness of Mrs Sefton in a series of poses which had obviously culminated in the more detailed painting on the easel which Goddard had seen yesterday. The very same painting on which Arthur Leon had been working just before someone had barged in and blasted him with a shotgun into the great and eternal atelier in the sky. Who?

Goddard went through the sketch pads once more, not really sure of what he was looking for. A clue, sure. But there wasn't any. Only a few landscapes and the nude drawings of the Sefton ladies. There was no doubt in Goddard's mind about those faces, the Seftons alright. There was only one faceless sketch — a female torso, neck to navel. Nice, demure almost. The upper part of the picture, where the face should have been, was charred and crumbled away so all Goddard really had in clear detail were the breasts and the little gold or silver chain around the neck and the curious little locket or ornament dangling from the chain and nestling in the cleavage. Curious, for a number of reasons – one, because there was no jewellery evident in any of the other sketches; two, because in this case the item of jewellery seemed to be the focal point, or the subject of the drawing, and it was pencilled and shaded in great detail whereas the anatomical features were just a few deft, brief strokes; and three, because the design of the ornament was one usually seen on a finger ring in Ireland, known as the Claddagh ring, two hands clasping a heart which is surmounted by a crown, the whole assembly symbolising Love, Fidelity and Honour.

Goddard had never seen one on a neck chain before. He wondered if Leon had given it to one of his mistresses as a gift, a love token maybe. Love, Fidelity and Honour? Not a very appropriate emblem to judge by the late Mr Leon's lifestyle, Goddard mused. And if he had given it to one of his mistresses, then which one? From the pencil lines depicting a slim waist and shoulders and small, neat, firm breasts Goddard guessed it had to be the teenager Karen. So what did that mean — had the stepmother found out about the gift and about Leon's two-timing? The echo of Karen Sefton's words came back to him. *You jealous old bitch! You killed him!* she'd

screamed at her step-mother. And then at her father —
*Blind fool! Behind your back she was having it off with
Arthur ....*

The possibility of discovering anything further or
worthwhile in the sketch pads — any sort of definite clue
or lead — faded into nothingness, into the grey damp
dawn and the haze of Goddard's own uncertainties.

'Did you find anything of interest?'

Startled, and frightened, Goddard spun around.

The brunette was standing only a few paces from him.
She was relaxed, calm, matter-of-fact, her hands thrust
deep into the pockets of her yellow windcheater. Where
had she crept from?

'Well?' she asked, indicating the sketch books. A faint,
enigmatic smile played at the corner of her mouth.

Goddard closed the books quickly, unzipped the front
of his anorak, placed the books flat against his stomach,
and then zipped up the anorak tightly. 'What the hell are
you doing here?' he snapped.

'Same as you. Snooping.'

'Yeah?' He was still tense. 'Find anything interesting?'

'Yes,' she nodded. 'Very interesting ....'

'What?'

She indicated the slight bulge caused by the sketch
pads. 'You show me yours and I'll show you mine.'

Goddard was in no mood for innuendo or teasing
games: 'What did you find. Show me.'

'Very well. Follow me.'

She led him across the wet grass and round the back
of the gutted building to a small shed or outhouse. Goddard hadn't noticed it before. It too had suffered extensive
fire damage. The blackened stone walls were still standing
but the roof had caved in. 'There,' she said simply.

He followed the direction of her pointed finger and —

'Oh Christ!' he groaned.

The body lying there — the upper part inside the doorway and partially covered by debris from the collapsed roof, the lower part outside — was Medwin's. There could be no mistaking the blue-and-white baseball cap in the muddy ashes and the checkerboard slacks. Goddard swore as he took an involuntary step towards the body and leaned over it. 'Is he ....?

'Dead? I'm afraid so. Poor Mr Medwin.'

'Yesterday Leon,' again he groaned. 'Now this. And each time I have to be the one to find the murdered body ....'

'Correction, Mr Goddard. I found this one. And, if it's any help, I don't think Mr Medwin was murdered.'

'No?'

'No. In my opinion he was trying to enter, slipped suddenly in the mud — you see this long skid mark leading to his shoe — lost his balance, his shoulder striking heavily against the rotted, or charred door post — see the ashy marks on his upper arm and shoulder? — and the lintel, already cracked from the heat, collapsed, bringing the whole lot down on him.'

'You're a regular little Sherlock Holmes,' he scowled, turning away from the sight of Medwin's crushed skull.

'That's what archaeology is mostly about. Observing, reading clues.'

'Don't give me any of that archaeology bullshit! What are you doing out here anyway?'

'I told you. The same as you, looking for the truth.'

'Yeah,' he scoffed, the set of his features showing his disbelief. 'Don't forget I'm a suspect. I'm involved ....'

'So am I, in a way.' She followed him out into the wan daylight. 'Look, Mr Goddard, I want to help you. If you and I were to co-operate and pool our knowledge of —'

'That's what *he* said!' Goddard jerked his head back in the direction of the corpse. 'Look what it got him! Jesus, for all I know I might be next!'

'Not if we work together.'

'Medwin said that too!'

'Medwin is dead. And Medwin was barking up the wrong tree.'

'What wrong tree?'

'Art forgeries. Fakes.'

'So, you *were* listening outside my door last night. Medwin was right.'

'Medwin was wrong, on just about everything.'

'You haven't answered my question.'

'You didn't ask one.'

'Okay, then I'm going to ask one — were you listening outside the door?'

'Yes,' she nodded, matter-of-factly. 'Not intentionally, at first. But Medwin has — sorry, *had* — a rather loud voice. Just about anyone passing in the corridor could have heard snatches of his talk. Art swindles, Sefton, forgeries, all that sort of thing.'

He thought about it for a few moments. They had crossed the lawn and were approaching the front gate and the lane. Ahead lay the village and Garda Muldowney. He paused.

'Alright,' he conceded reluctantly, 'and you say he was wrong about all that stuff?'

'Uh-huh.'

'How?'

She shook her head, and a tentative smile returned briefly to her lips: 'I showed you mine ....' She nodded back towards where Medwin lay, and then with the same nod indicated the bulge inside his anorak, '... now you show me yours, okay?'

'Why should I?'

'Because sooner or later, Mr Goddard, we're going to have to put what we have together.'

What way did she mean that? The pleasurable conjecture dissolved rapidly when he suddenly considered the mess he was in — less than twenty-four hours on a rain-swept godforsaken fucking island, two dead bodies, his presence at the scene of both discoveries, and a thousand and one other unanswered questions and bloody fucking possibilities!

'Before I show you or anybody *anything* ....' he snapped, jabbing his forefinger before her face, 'you better start telling me what you — you and poor fucking Medwin! — were doing out here at this godforsaken hour in this godforsaken kip!'

'Curiosity,' she replied simply, opening the gate for him and leading him out onto the laneway. 'In my case, I woke up some hours ago with the realisation that perhaps the heavy rain may have put out the fire, and perhaps it might not be such a bad idea to come out and have a look round. I presume that much the same thing may have occurred to both you and the late Mr Medwin. In his case, unfortunately, curiosity killed the cat.'

'And in my case?'

She shrugged slightly, again with the beginning of that faint, enigmatic smile: 'In your case, I think, a propensity to hide your uncertainties under a wagging forefinger ...?'

He quickly shoved his hands into the pockets of his anorak. 'Okay, let's head back to town and report all this crap — Medwin's body, the accident — to Muldowney. Oh, Jesus ....'

'Don't worry too much about Garda Muldowney,' she said in the same calm and infuriatingly reassuring tone. 'I'll deal with him.'

He stomped ahead of her for a few paces, almost angry. Then, relenting a little, he slowed down until she was more or less level with him. They walked side by side in silence for a few minutes.

'By the way, my name is Kelly. Ashling Kelly ....'

'Goddard. Joe Goddard.'

'Yes, I know. May I call you Joe?'

'Be my guest.' He hunched his shoulders with feigned indifference.

She withdrew a slim white hand from the pocket of her windcheater and extended it towards him. 'You may call me Ashling, if you like ...?'

He hesitated for a moment, then reached out and shook her hand. What did that mean exactly? Were they just two hotel residents politely exchanging names and becoming acquainted? Or becoming some kind of allies? Was he allowing himself to be manoeuvred, used ... drifting deeper into the spreading pool of mystery and suspicion, getting out of his depth?

Despite himself, and still somewhat confused, he felt oddly encouraged by her air of calm assurance, competence — attractiveness, maybe? He suddenly unzipped the anorak and withdrew the sketch pads.

'Before I give you these — mind you, there's nothing very much in them from what I can see, so what the hell! — Anyway, what's all this about Medwin barking up the wrong tree?'

'Not art forgeries, Joe. That's old hat.' She accepted the proferred sketch pads with an appreciative nod. 'Sefton moved out of that field about three years ago, and covered his tracks exceedingly well. Oh he was certainly involved, but there's nothing that will stand up in court, I'm afraid.'

'How do you know so much about all this?'

Engrossed in her examination of the sketches — or pretending to be? – Ashling Kelly didn't answer. She went on: 'If there was anything at all still lying around Owls Watch that might possibly have linked him with

Leon's forgeries then Sefton took care of that yesterday.'

'The fire? What makes you so sure it was Sefton?'

'I saw him drive up just after you and Miss Fontana hurried away from the cottage. I was out hill walking and—'

'Of much more importance right now is whether you saw anyone entering the cottage *before* Gloria and I got there —'

'*Gloria?*' She flashed a brief, sidelong glance at him, part curious appraisal, part teasing smile.

'Miss Fontana, then,' he muttered impatiently. 'Just stick to the point. Did you see who was at the cottage *before* us? Whoever may have killed Leon?'

"Fraid not.'

'You're sure?'

'Uh-huh.'

'Could it have been Sefton?'

'I doubt it. If he had killed Leon — for whatever reason — and had intended to set fire to the place, surely he would have started the blaze there and then? He'd hardly drive home for lunch or whatever and then return some time later to finish the job. It doesn't make sense, does it?'

Goddard considered that for a few moments: 'Okay, so you think that Sefton, just like myself and Gloria — Miss Fontana — happened on Leon's corpse by accident and then, for reasons best known to himself, suddenly decided to set the place alight.'

'Something like that,' she nodded. She was still keeping pace with him while carefully going through the pages of the sketch book. 'Nice. Very nice, wouldn't you say?'

She tilted a nude study of Karen Sefton — all splayed limbs, saucy, erotic — for Goddard's inspection. He made no comment. She laughed lightly: 'I'm beginning to see why Leon may have put Sefton onto the Sheela-na-Gigs.'

'Sheela-na-*what?*'

'Sheela-na-gig — an ancient stone carving depicting a naked female with exaggerated genitalia. The role of the Sheelae-na-gigs in Celtic and early Christian legend is obscure, though some experts think they may have been used to "frighten" the devil away from church sites. Others, because of the Norman use of —'

'What the hell has that got to do with Sefton?'

'Quite a lot. Don't you see, Joe, there's a network of treasure hunters who are making a lucrative living out of illegally selling Irish antiquities on the international market. It's big business. Millions annually.'

'And you're telling me that Sefton switched from trafficking in art fakes to the genuine stuff?'

'Yes, I think so —'

'You *think* — you've no proof?'

'Not yet, but I'm almost certain ....'

'*Almost* — Jesus!'

'I'm ninety-five per cent positive.'

'But not a hundred!'

'Not yet. Not exactly. Look Joe, Sefton — from his art forgery days — already has his own international contacts. A network of unscrupulous dealers. He's a middleman. A fence, if you like.'

'But you've no bloody *proof*! Meanwhile I'm the prime suspect in a murder case and —'

'True, but ....'

'But me no buts, Kelly! I'm like a shit on a swing-swong — I don't know if I'm coming or going!'

'Will you just listen, please!' She closed the sketch books with a snap as she hurried to keep up with his angry stride. 'Just listen — look, I think you can help us to convict Sefton and at the same time prove your own innocence.'

'Who's *us?*'

She hesitated momentarily, biting her lip. 'There isn't too much time left. Joe. We're going to have to trust one another.'

'Who the fuck is *us*?'

'Okay,' she conceded, placing a restraining hand on his arm. 'Okay Joe. Us — *we* — are a small handful of committed archaeologists, friends of the National Museum, and liaising with the Museum staff, who know for a fact that highly organised gangs — not to mention weekend metal detector enthusiasts, sub-aqua explorers, amateur historians and all that lot! — but *highly* organised gangs, some of whom have para-military connections, are almost daily ransacking our heritage of —'

'First it's *us*! Now it's *ours*!'

'... Vandalising and robbing our archaeological artefacts!'

'What sort of damned arte —?'

'Just listen, for Christ sake!' There was a steely side to Ashling Kelly that he hadn't noticed before. 'Artefacts such as pre-historic weapons, gravestones, coins, Bronze Age trinkets, Viking swords, religious manuscripts, Armada cannons, Gaelic brooches, lunulae, just about everything of our past! Our heritage, in short ....' Her large, dark eyes were moist, almost tearful.

He pulled up suddenly and, as she attempted to sweep past him, he reached out and grabbed her arm, forcing her to swing round and meet his gaze. All his anger was gone.

'You're really serious about all this shit, aren't you?'

'What *shit*?' she flared.

'Sorry,' he made a feeble, apologetic wave with his free hand. Then he tried to tack a contrite grin onto the end of the gesture. 'I didn't mean shit. It's just that I couldn't think of an appropriate collective noun for Viking swords, gravestones, coins and all that sh—stuff. But it really does bother you, Kelly, doesn't it?'

She met his eyes, nodding affirmatively, blinking back what might just have been the beginning — or the end? — of a giveaway tear.

'Why?' He tried to broaden his grin.

'Why what?'

'Why does it bother you?'

'Because ...' When she made a slight shrug a tiny hint of vulnerability peeped through the earlier self-assurance, '... because all that shit, as you so inelegantly put it, belongs to you Joe ... and to me, and to our children ....'

'*Our* children?' He winked. Now that he was momentarily in control he felt like doing the teasing.

'Future generations of Irish children, I mean ....'

'I know what you meant, Kelly,' he smiled, taking her hand sympathetically. 'Don't worry, I'll help you nail Sefton.'

'I know what you mean Goddard.' She too essayed a kind of smile, briefly squeezing his hand. 'Don't worry, I'll help you beat a murder rap.'

But, Goddard thought, could he keep his promise? Could he nail Sefton? More importantly, could Ashling Kelly help him beat a murder rap?

Under the gathering rain clouds they walked down towards the harbour and the main street.

7

'What first put you onto Sefton?' he asked, as he accepted the sketch pads back from her, zipping them safely away once more.

'A number of things.' She too was zipping up and pulling the yellow hood of her jacket up round the dark hair and against the first broad spatters of rain. 'Most of our archaeological sites are open to the public, so that everything of value that is not protected is a vulnerable target. Expert thieves are using published guides and books about Ireland's national monuments as "hit lists" when planning raids ....'

'Kelly, could you please get to the point. What about Sefton?'

'A few years ago Sefton bought a building site as close as possible to the old monastic ruins here. These ruins appear in very few of the guide books, old or modern. And that's where he had the Laurels built.'

'So?'

'So that, together with the relative seclusion of the Laurels at the most inaccessible part of one of the most remote islands on our western coast, leads me to believe that he planned to have exclusive and almost undisturbed rights to plundering the ruins. Two days ago I discovered some signs that someone was over the place with a metal detector — probably during the winter and early spring — and there's certainly evidence of near-expert camouflaging of diggings.'

'But that's all you have to go on?'

'Not quite. Sean Muldowney informs me that all this summer the Seftons have been doing a great deal of scuba-diving in the cove beside their home.'

'An Armada wreck?'

'Could be, though the Armada archives in Spain and Admiralty records in London, plus our own researches here, don't seem to indicate such a wreck. But there's another possibility.'

'What's that?'

'In the 16th century a raiding party of Elizabethan soldiers destroyed the monastery. Perhaps before their arrival the monks hastily buried — or consigned to the sea? — some of their most precious items, with a view to recovering them at a later date. But the monks were either killed, dispersed, or imprisoned. At any rate they never returned.'

'And you suspect that the Seftons, between diving and metal detecting techniques, are collecting the treasure and quietly stowing it away for future export and sale?'

'Exactly.'

'If you're so sure of all this, and if you've already had some discussion of it with Muldowney, why don't you just get a search warrant?'

She nodded at the logic of that, but added her own question: 'You're a newspaperman Joe, right?'

'Sort of ....'

'And when you feel you're onto a scoop, an exclusive story, don't you try to check out all the facts, all the sources, before going off half-cocked?'

'Sure, but ....'

'But me no buts, Goddard,' she smiled. 'Most archaeologists are just the same as newspaper folk. The responsible ones don't like to end up with egg on their faces by going off half-cocked.'

'Touche. But why not hand over all your information — your suspicions or evidence, or whatever — to the police and let them sort it out?'

'Well, in a way, I am. Sean Muldowney and I have started to keep in touch on this matter —'

'Oh terrific! And what does the rustic Hercule Poirot think?'

She brushed that aside: 'First I've *got* to have a good look around Sefton's place. Not just outside. Inside. And that's where you can help.'

'Me? How?'

Ashling Kelly flashed another of her strange little smiles and pointed down the rain-swept street. Goddard followed her gaze. In the bleak morning light, and through the steady curtains of rain sweeping back and forth, it was deserted — except for the view of Sefton's car parked outside Sean Muldowney's lodgings-cum-police station.

'And now, if all goes according to ...' she muttered in the same even, matter-of-fact tone, a kind of quiet soliloquy that was almost drowned out by the increasing rain sounds, before resuming in a louder voice, '... if all goes the way I *think* it will, then our Mr Sefton should be calling to the hotel about breakfast time with a most cordial invitation to you and the Widow Leon — sorry, *Gloria* !— to join him and his family at the Laurels for lunch and tennis, or billiards, or —'

'Why the hell would he want to do that?' Behind the question Goddard was wondering if she had been about to say 'if all goes according to plan'. Who's plan? Her's? Sefton's? Muldowney's? Nothing from his past experiences

— nothing that happened since coming here, was of much use in helping him to cope. He couldn't put anything, or any of the questions, together. In a low voice that lacked finality he repeated: 'Why on earth would he want to invite me?'

'Not just *you*. Also Miss What's-her-name ...?'

'Gloria. Miss Fontana.'

'Both of you. Ostensibly he'll want to offer his sympathy to the widow of his late friend and neighbour, and — as you seem to be her, shall I say, friend, companion, *comforter*? — anyway, he'll want to offer you both the finest hospitality and the best amusements this dreary little island can offer. Especially as you are two distressed, bored, grieving, disorientated tourists cooped up in a dismal rain-swept hotel, so to speak. But in reality Sefton will be chafing at the bit to politely — and charmingly! — question you both about *everything* you may have seen or discovered at Owls Watch before it went up in smoke.'

'But if he lit the match and burnt down the place with whatever clues might link him to Leon, why would he bother wasting time grilling Gloria and me?'

'Because he'll learn absolutely *nothing* from Sean Muldowney. In fact, Muldowney will imply that you and Miss What's-her-name, together with your photographs as evidence, have unearthed a virtual can of worms, all sorts of clues and connections. And he'll do so, without giving anything of his own thoughts away. He'll do it through a smokescreen of his usual local proverbs and seemingly slow-witted homespun philosophy. He'll do it — like the clever, local fisherman that he is — by setting the right bait and attracting the right fish.'

'You seem to know a lot about Muldowney?'

The brief, affirmative shake of her head was followed by an equally brief smile that was either affectionate or whimsical; Goddard couldn't tell which. She simply said:

'I'd say that just about now Sean Muldowney is quietly implanting the idea in our Mr Sefton's mind that two hapless visitors marooned on a rain-sodden island, and cooped up in a miserable hotel, would gladly and willingly ....' and here Ashling Kelly essayed a tolerably good imitation of Muldowney's skull-scratching gesture and accent, '... "would willingly welcome a bit of warm-hearted civility and daycent hospitality and divarshun from a fine gentleman such as your good self an' yo'r lovely family, so that they might be free to unburden themselves from the awful happenin's to a sympathetic an' kindly patron" ....' Then her accent, and play-acting suddenly changed. 'And this is where you can help me, Joe.'

'How?'

'By insisting — if such an invitation is forthcoming from Sefton — that there are *three* hapless visitors marooned on a rain-sodden island and cooped up in a miserable hotel. That you *want* me to be along too.'

'But supposing Sefton says "no"?'

'You'll have to think of something, Joe! Tell him — tell him that you have an appointment with me, a date that you can't break — anything! Insist that you must have me with you. I *have* to get into the Laurels!'

'Gloria mightn't like the idea of —'

'To hell with Gloria!' she said, vehemently. 'I have to get into the Laurels! And you need me on your side if you want to prove you're innocence.'

He nodded glumly: 'That reminds me, I've got to report Medwin's death to Muldowney ....'

'Leave Sean Muldowney to me. Just concentrate on having me invited along with you and What's-her-name! *Please*, Joe!' Her expression was all entreaty.

'Yeah, but ....'

'But me no buts.'

'... Medwin's body ...?'

'You're already down for one dead body. Have Medwin's on me, okay?' Then, with the rain suddenly squalling around them, she reached up, her hand encircling his neck, drawing his face down to meet her's. She kissed him on the mouth. Not perfunctorily, but slowly. After a few moments the tip of her tongue began to explore the corner of his lips as her body almost moulded itself against his, fighting the wind-driven rain.

Just before his arms had time to lock her into this incongruous embrace she quickly drew back, her eyes still smiling entreatingly ....

'The *three* of us, Joe, okay? You, me and What's-her-name ...?'

All he saw was the diamond points of moisture on her dark hair under the yellow hood, diamond points glistening like her eyes.

'Yeah ... yes, Kelly, whatever you say ....'

Then she suddenly detached herself and was hurrying across the narrow, wet street towards Muldowney's office, turning once to wave at him.

There was no one else about at this hour, in this rain, so he knew that the kiss and the wave — and the whole insouciant performance! — was intended solely for Sefton's eyes.

Sefton had been watching them — for how long? — watching and peering from behind the rivulets of rain running down Muldowney's window.

Goddard trudged towards the shelter of the hotel.

He had a quick clean-up, a shave and a change into dry clothes before coming back down for breakfast. He took the window seat this time, hoping to keep an eye on Muldowney's office. Was Ashling Kelly still there? Sefton's car was still outside, gleaming in the downpour.

'Morning Mr Goddard. Isn't the weather just too awful for words? Mammy says it's going to last *all* day,' Murty whinnied disconsolately. When Goddard, too preoccupied with his own thoughts, remained silent Murty relapsed into his mildly miffed tone: 'May I take your order now sir — continental or full breakfast?'

'The works, Murty.' The walk to and from Owls Watch had given him an appetite. Murty gave a curt nod and flounced kitchen-wards.

Gloria joined Goddard when he was almost finished his bacon and eggs. She looked radiant, a blue sailor-type outfit with white trimmings and a ribbon of the same blue worked delicately through her fluffed-out hair.

'Hi,' she smiled. 'Sleep well?'

'Uh-huh,' Goddard lowered his voice. 'Where did you get to after …?'

'Back to my own room,' Gloria continued to smile, but didn't lower her voice. 'I didn't want to compromise you.' Under the table she took his hand and squeezed it. 'Hey, I forgot to ask you — are you married?'

He shook his head: 'Would it have made any difference?'

'Not last night, it wouldn't ….' Still holding his hand she brought it up from beneath the table and raised it to her lips. 'It's just that I wouldn't want to do any poaching or ….'

'Cut it out. Here's Murty.'

'Ah, so you've got a thing going with the house maid,' she whispered, releasing his hand.

Gloria ordered fruit juice, pot of coffee and one slice of toast. 'At my game you've got to watch the calories.'

When Murty was gone she reached for Goddard's hand once more. 'Know something Joe … I feel like a honeymooner.'

'Sorry Gloria. I think the honeymoon is just about to end.

She followed his gaze to the diningroom door. Sefton had just appeared there and was coming straight towards them. His forceful stride and handsome, assertive self-confidence seemed strangely at variance with his expression of extremely polite apology. Something just wasn't right, Goddard guessed. The self-confidence or the apology?

'I do beg your pardon for this unwarranted intrusion. No, please don't get up ....' He laid a strong, patronising hand on Goddard's shoulder, almost dismissing him as he turned the full charm of a pained and solicitous frown on Gloria: 'Do forgive me, but I have only just learned that you were Arthur's wife ....'

'Ex-wife.'

'Yes. Quite so. Nonetheless, under these most tragic circumstances, I just had to come at once and offer my most sincere condolences.'

'Thank you ... but Arty and me hadn't really ... I mean, for the past few years we didn't ....'

Sefton had already taken her hand in one of his, and now he silenced her by clasping his second hand over hers, overpowering her with a gesture of heartfelt sympathy and the words: 'Arthur, God rest him, was one of my dearest friends. One of my *very* dearest friends. I too share your grief. And, my dear young lady, I fully realise what a terrible shock this terrible tragedy must be to you. May I sit down?'

As Sefton drew over a chair from another table Goddard tried to regain the edge by muttering: 'I think maybe the dear young lady might prefer ....'

'Yes, I know exactly what the young lady must be feeling at this moment. A shocking, shocking tragedy! Undoubtedly a great blow to you. Which brings me to the purpose of my visit here – my unpardonable intrusion at this moment — but I wish, in these sad circumstances, to offer you, Mrs Leon ....'

'I'm Miss Fontana now ....'

'... Miss Fontana, yes. Yes, quite so. I wish to offer you, Miss Fontana, not only my condolences and the condolences of my family, but also our sympathetic hospitality at the Laurels. Oh, and you too of course, Mr —?'

'Goddard. Joe Goddard.'

'... You too Mr Goddard, naturally. I can appreciate how it must be for both of you cooped up here in a rather dismal hotel, in this weather, and after Arthur's tragic death .... Oh, by the way, perhaps I should introduce myself. Jack Sefton's the name.'

'We met yesterday, Mr Sefton,' Goddard said, playing with his tea cup. 'At Owls Watch. Remember?'

'Yes. Yes, of course.' For a moment Sefton looked grave, his broad handsome face and greying temples lowered into semi-shadows. Then he raised his head, and with a gesture of his well-manicured hands which seemed to appeal for some appreciation of his problems, he resumed: 'Which brings me to another matter. I refer, of course, to the matter of my family's behaviour at that terrible scene. They were quite distraught, you understand. A terrible shock, really.'

'For everyone,' Goddard nodded, encouraging Sefton to go on.

'Yes, for everyone. Naturally. But my wife and my daughter ... Arthur was a great friend of ours, you understand, and he could be so charming, so gallant ... my daughter Karen was understandably quite infatuated. Perfectly natural at her impressionable age.'

'Perfectly,' Gloria mumbled.

'My wife too, I suppose in her own way. Not that I was in any way jealous, let me hasten to add ....'

'No?' Goddard sensed a small advantage.

'No. On the contrary ....' Sefton was in command

again; he continued brightly: 'I'm a man of business. I'm abroad a lot. I frankly confess that I don't always give my family the time and attention they have a right to expect. Oh certainly I provide them with all material comforts — this place on the island, for instance, an apartment in London, a little place in Scotland, that sort of thing — well, I think you know what I mean ....'

'Sure,' Goddard said off-handedly.

'I never minded the little attentions that Arthur paid to them. The little gallantries, flirtations. In fact whenever I was abroad I was always quite relieved to know that they were in such good hands, so to speak. Arthur was most attentive.'

'I can imagine,' Gloria pushed the coffee pot towards Sefton and gestured towards a clean cup and saucer on the next table.

He shook his head, resuming: 'As I said, my daughter Karen was quite infatuated. Understandably so. And my wife — by the way, I should explain that Helen is my second wife, and therefore is not Karen's mother — well, I'm quite sure you can imagine how things sometimes are between a step-mother and a spoiled daughter. Oh yes, I freely confess that I rather spoiled Karen when she was younger ....'

'Why are you telling us all this?' Goddard asked bluntly.

'You see Miss Fontana,' Sefton went on, ignoring Goddard's question, 'I commissioned Arthur — your dear late husband, my very dearest friend — to paint a portrait of my wife. I need hardly tell you that he was an excellent painter. A real, genuine talent ....'

'In the style of the Old Masters,' Goddard raised his teacup in salute.

'... And as my wife, Helen, frequently went to Owls Watch for sittings, as you can appreciate ... well, Karen unfortunately misconstrued the purpose of those visits ....'

'Unfortunately.'

'... Hence the little *contretemps* yesterday.' He suddenly turned his man-to-man smile on Goddard: 'You know what some women are like in times of emotional shock, times of sudden tragedy ....'

'Sure,' Goddard responded with a 'we-men-of-the-world' wink, 'I know how it is Mr Sefton.'

'Call me Jack.' He placed a hand on Goddard's shoulder, smiling cordially. 'And now, as much for my family's sake as mine, I would consider it a great honour if you two young people would be kind enough to accept my invitation ....' Sefton, still smiling confidently, looked from one to the other.

'No can do, I'm afraid,' Goddard shook his head.

'I beg your pardon?'

'Thanks, but I've promised to spend the afternoon with Miss Kelly ....' He avoided Gloria's swift glance. 'Unless of course you'd care to invite her along as well?'

'What's all this about Miss Kelly?' Gloria asked. 'Who's she?'

'Ah,' Sefton nodded, the smile fading. 'The young lady I met just a short time ago in Muldowney's office, eh?'

'Who is she?' Gloria's question was directed at Goddard.

'A friend. I met her out walking this morning. We made arrangements for this afternoon. How about it Jack?'

Sefton hesitated.

'There's only three guests staying here. Three, that's all. You were saying something about being cooped up in this dismal hotel ....' He hoped Murty and Mammy were out of earshot! '... so why leave one out?'

'I was really only thinking of yourself and Miss Fontana, due to the shock you both must have experienced on discovering poor Arthur's body ....'

'Oh if finding dead bodies qualifies for the invitation then there's no problem. Miss Kelly found Medwin's. Didn't Muldowney tell you?'

'Medwin — *the Yank*?' Gloria dropped a spoon and sat there open-mouthed.

'Yes, Muldowney told me.' Sefton suddenly got up from his chair. There was a kind of capitulation in the movement. 'Very well then, in view of the fact that you seem to have had a prior engagement with Miss Kelly. Three it is then. I'll trust you to convey my sincere invitation to her as well. Okay?'

'Thanks Jack, 'preciate it ....'

Sefton turned away, taking Gloria's hand and bowing over it: 'Will noon be alright? Good. I'll have Karen pick you up here.'

Without another word, or a glance at Goddard, he marched out of the room as splendidly as he'd marched in just a short time before.

'Medwin — Jeez!' Gloria repeated, shaking her head from side to side.

'Dead as a doornail.'

'Murdered?'

'Could be, but Kelly doesn't think so ....'

'*Kelly* — the goody-two-shoes with the glasses and the books?'

Goddard didn't answer. Ashling Kelly — as though she'd been waiting outside for Sefton's departure — was now framed in the doorway. She stood there for just a moment, looking across at Goddard with a 'how did we do' question in her eyes.

He raised his hand, making a little circle of his forefinger and thumb and winked at her.

'What the fuck is going on here?' Gloria snapped.

8

The rain was unremitting, shrouding the hills in darkness. It came in various shapes, sweeping in from the Atlantic under black clouds, in dark diagonals hammering on the roof of the car, in pools of water sloshing up out of the roadway potholes, in slashing curtains across the windscreen.

Goddard wished Miss Karen Sefton would pay a bit more attention to the winding road. She kept turning round now and then to address the back-seat passengers, Ashling and Gloria — or (Goddard wryly considered) to judge from their broody near-silences, Miss Goody-Two-Shoes and Miss What's-her-Name. He was in the front, alongside the glamorous chatterbox.

'And what about you Mr Goddard? Daddy tells me you're a real swinging up-market photographer ....'

'Real swinging up-market, that's me.'

'Gosh! *Really*! Think you could get me into one of those glossies, *Playboy*, *Cosmopolitan*, *Woman's Journal*? 'Course Daddy or the Dragon Lady would never allow me pose for anything *too* saucy. You know, topless or anything ....' She giggled, all sun-tanned and white teeth and fluttering lashes. 'Arty used to say — O*ops*! So sorry Mrs

Leon! ... Gosh, I could just bite my tongue off ...!'

'Go ahead,' Gloria muttered.

'... Some *people* say I've just the right figure for a real fashion model.'

'I've no doubt about it Karen,' Goddard smiled, eyeing the long denim-clad legs beside him.

'Think so? *Really?*'

'Really.'

'Super! I think I might get into my bikini. Hey, do you have a camera with you?'

'Uh-huh. Part of my permanent equipment, almost.'

'Terrific! How about it girls, photo sessions by the pool? You can borrow some of my stuff. I've absolutely any amount. That is, of course, if it fits. I'm a ten. Oops, sorry, no swimming though. The pool is sort of out of bounds today. Daddy says it's something to do with the heating or the filtration or some such crap.'

'What a pity,' Kelly said, getting into the conversation for the first time. 'I was really looking forward to a swim. What's the pool like Miss Sefton?'

'Call me Karen. The pool? Oh, you know, sort of natural like. Boulders all round the patio area, stony bottom, that sort of thing. Well, not *entirely* natural if you know what I mean. Daddy had it kind of specially designed, but retaining most of the natural features. At the deep end it's about fifteen foot. Good diving there. And all natural sea water too. Underwater there's a kind of sluice gate gadgety thingamagig that kind of seals in one tide, and then can be opened to let the water out again. Pity about the swimming girls, huh? But Daddy is sort of strict about things like that. Safety, you know. Still, if Mr Goddard — hey, can I call you Joe?'

'Sure.'

'If Joe has his camera, no reason why we can't get into our swimwear and pose beside the pool. A few pretend shots on the diving board, that sort of thing. It's all got a kind of sun roof thing over it, so we'll be out of the rain. How about it girls? Maybe Joe'll get our pictures into one of those flashy magazines, huh? Of course ....' Karen simpered self-deprecatingly, 'As I said, I'm only a ten and kind of younger, so maybe ...?' She left the challenge dangling as the car swept in through the open gateway. 'Well, here we are!'

Waiting to meet them at the open front door, and holding a large golf umbrella, was a white-tunicked Oriental type. Filipino, Chinese, Japanese? Goddard wasn't too sure, but he guessed the squat young foreigner with the beaming smile to be the Sefton's butler-cum-houseboy. The umbrella seemed superfluous in view of the fact that the station wagon screeched to a halt under the protective canopy of a broad carport and just a few inches short of the rear fender of the parked black Toyota which Goddard had seen earlier that morning outside Muldowney's place.

Karen Sefton leaped out of the driver's seat and with a swift, long-legged pirouette opened the back door for Ashling Kelly. Goddard, much slower, got out on his side and fumbled with the door handle to release Gloria while his eyes swivelled round to take in his immediate surroundings. Through the wavering curtains of rain streaming down from the carport roof he glimpsed, in the foreground and only a few hundred yards from him, the gable end of a small church, portion of a carved cross, a stump of what appeared to have been a round tower and a scattering of old and discarded stones — all of which, he surmised, must mark the site of the ancient monastery mentioned by Ashling Kelly. The background was shrouded in rainy near-darkness.

As she uncoiled herself from the back seat of the car Gloria hissed: 'What the hell are we doing in this kip? The place is so bleedin' spooky ....'

'We've got to beat a murder rap, remember?' he whispered, making a tentative grab at her arm as she shivered past him.

'Yeah? How — by ogling teeny-boppers? Cut the crap Joe!' The shiver became a flounce as Gloria hurried round the back of the car and up the two or three steps to join Karen Sefton.

At the same time the little Oriental guy was coming down the steps, bowing to everyone in turn, smiling with something akin to obsequiousness while unfurling the large umbrella, and then hurrying out from under the carport canopy and down towards the front gate. For just a few moments Goddard continued his professional study of the ruined monastery and the bleak landscape beyond it. He was considering the possibility of a few 'atmospheric' shots — even fiddling with the leather covering of his camera — when he suddenly felt Ashling Kelly's hand on his arm.

'Not now Joe,' she murmured. 'I think they're waiting for us.'

'Huh? Oh yeah,' then, matching her murmur, he added: 'I'm not sure what we're letting ourselves in for, but you have to admit I got the three of us here like you asked.'

'And you're handling the three of us perfectly. Me, Miss What's-her-name and the bimbo. How do you think you'll do with Mamma?'

'Mamma?'

'Mrs Sefton.'

'No problem Kelly. You heard the bimbo, I'm a real swinging up-market guy.'

'Then you better start swinging.' Ashling glanced over her shoulder by way of explanation. 'Here comes the Dragon Lady.'

But Goddard didn't follow her gaze. His eyes were rivetted on the white-coated fellow under the umbrella. Despite the rain cascading down from the flimsy rim of the umbrella and making a kind of inverted halo of puddles about his feet the servant was carefully affixing a kind of padlock to the gate he had just closed. Were they being locked in? Why?

The little guy in the impeccably white jacket served lunch — a sumptuous affair of salmon steaks, seafood platters, exotic salads, cheese and expensive wines. The diningroom was spacious, mock-English Manor style, with muted wall lighting from imitation lanterns glinting on the varnish of great oaken pillars that supported a beamed ceiling of the same wood. The muted light made tiny glitters on the table silver and cut-glass decanters. The panels on the lower half of the walls were of the same black oak, and the floor, its polished boards mostly covered by a scattering of fine rugs, appeared to be composed of the same material. Decorating the rough-hewn stone of the chimney breast were the horns of a stag. Beneath it was a big open fireplace of crackling logs. A long window — almost the entire length of one wall — gave out onto an angry sea and kept out the snarl of the wind-driven rain splattering and coursing down the thick glass.

Sefton was the perfect host: charming, witty, painstaking in his attention to the needs of his guests, regaling them with humorous anecdotes, finger-snapping the guy in the white jacket to replenish glasses, take away plates, pass around new delights. He had an impressive, shoulder-shaking laugh, infectious if it had been genuine. But Goddard wasn't taken in by any of it. He viewed the massive dinner table as the ultimate barrier between himself and Sefton, the lace tablecloth like a snow-white battlefield, the cut-glass goblets and the silver and the candelabra deployed like so many strategic outposts before two opposing generals.

But if Goddard was a general, who were his allies? Gloria? For the most part she was silent, playing with her wine glass, answering in dull monosyllables. She was clearly uncomfortable. Ashling? She was more spirited, animated almost, despite the fact that she declined any further wine after the first glass. Goddard was glad of her frequent contributions to the pointless chit-chat.

From the opposite quarter — Sefton's side in terms of conversational allies, though Goddard found himself seated next to Mrs Sefton — most of the running was left to the host himself, with some support from his daughter. Mrs Sefton was all polite aloofness, confining herself to the minimum of small talk. She sipped steadily and had her glass refilled regularly. It was easy to imagine that she'd been against this whole lunch business from the very beginning. But Karen Sefton seemed glad of the company, plying Gloria with no end of questions about show business and being rewarded with terse, lacklustre responses for all her gushing enthusiasm.

Such small talk and pleasantries took up most of the meal-time. It wasn't until the coffee and liqueur stage that Sefton began to adroitly steer the conversation round into the matter of 'poor Arthur's tragic death', doing so, naturally, with appropriate expressions of sad regret and fulsome condolences. It was like a signal to break up. Goddard wondered if the shift of talk was deliberate.

'Please excuse me,' Helen Sefton said, her voice suddenly tremulous. 'I find all this talk of Arthur — I find it too distressing.' She stood up. 'Also, I think I've had a little too much wine. Forgive me ... No, please don't disturb yourselves. I think I'll lie down for a little while.

I feel a headache coming on. I'm sorry, I'll join you again in an hour or two ....'

Sefton was out of his chair and round the table with solicitous alacrity and leading his wife gently to the door.

'Come on girls,' Karen Sefton also rose — also taking her cue? — nodding and smiling at Gloria and Ashling, and finishing with a little wink. 'Change of life, you know how it is ....' she whispered across the table. 'What d'you say we leave the men to their cigars and brandy, okay? Anyway, I want to show you round the place. We've an indoor tennis court if you like ....'

'No thanks,' Gloria pushed back her chair. 'Think I could doss down somewhere for a siesta too? I'm not used to knocking back the juice so early in the day.'

In all the sudden movement Ashling Kelly had time to mutter: 'Keep Sefton here as long as possible Joe. I need time to have a good look-around. *Please?*'

Goddard wasn't too sure how he might manage that, but he nodded.

Karen Sefton, looking back over her shoulder and smiling, interpreted the affirmative nod as something intended for her. 'Yes, don't forget Joe. We've got a date for some photos, remember?'

'Sure, how could I forget.'

Sefton closed the door after the departing females. Returning, and collecting a brandy bottle and a cigar box from the sideboard en route, he smiled affably and motioned Goddard to join him at the fireside armchairs.

'Sorry about Helen. But you know how it is with women at that age. Also, she's fairly cut up about Arthur's death.' He flopped down in one of the throne-like chairs. 'But enough of such topics. I'd just like to say Joe that I can't remember when we've had such delightful company to lunch. Really delightful. Charming young ladies, your Miss Fontana and Miss Kelly.'

'Mine?'

'You know what I mean,' Sefton gave another of his 'us-men-of-the-world' nods. 'Must say I rather envy you. Charming young ladies. Tell me, Joe ....' Sefton leaned across and proferred the cigar box, 'Miss Kelly, is she an archaeologist or something?'

They'd been taking measure of each other for the past hour and a half and now Sefton was coming to the point. Goddard knew he'd have to fence, or shadow box. He delayed answering as he made a big thing of selecting a cigar.

'I'm a cigarette man really. Not often I get the chance of a really good cigar. Thanks ....'

'Havanas, specially imported,' Sefton muttered. 'Here, allow me.' He snipped the end of the cigar with practised ease and then lit it for Goddard. 'We were talking about Miss Kelly ....'

'Were we?'

'Yes. Miss Kelly — or Ashling, is it? — she was probing around the old monastery ruins next door, so to speak, a few days ago. I just wondered if she might have an interest in archaeology. Has she?'

'Archaeology? No, I don't think so,' Goddard lied easily through a rich puff of smoke. 'Botany maybe. I think she's a student. Very interested in flora and bog plants. You know, mosses and ferns and lichens, that kind of stuff.'

'I see. But I have the impression that she ....'

'Talking of probing around would you like to know what I found when I was poking around Owls Watch before the fire?' Goddard knew that Sefton was fishing, getting too close to Kelly's purposes; he was also remembering her whispered request to keep Sefton here as long as possible.

'You found something at Owls Watch?' Sefton was too off-hand, almost disinterested, as he poured a liberal measure of brandy into Goddard's glass. 'Cheers.'

'Cheers.' Goddard raised his glass. The splendid lunch and the warm glow induced by so much alcohol made him feel, no matter how desperate the situation, a certain sense of recklessness. 'Yeah, I found positive evidence of art forgeries at Owls Watch.'

For a moment Sefton looked grave, then he continued brightly: 'Oh, you mean Arthur's studio for dabbling in imitations of the Old Masters?'

'I mean Arthur's studio for the lucrative faking of Old Masters, yeah. No question about it Jack, Ole Arthur was onto a good money spinner. Did you know about it?'

'About Arthur's desire to master every aspect of painting, to emulate all the great painters of the past? Certainly I knew about it.' Sefton beamed, lolling back in his chair.

'About faking?'

'What exactly do you mean by faking, Joe?' Sefton swished the brandy about in the balloon glass, giving the impression of a man in complete control. 'Let me explain a few facts to you, Joe. Painting fakes isn't a crime, *per se*. To paint a picture in the manner of Van Gogh, say, or Matisse, and to sign it, to doctor it up so that it looks old, even down to doodling authentic looking inscriptions on the back of the canvas in order to add the deceptive impression that the work in question is by Van Gogh — none of that is criminal. The problem — the crime, if you like — comes when the painting is put up for sale as a supposed original.'

'And isn't that what Leon was doing?'

'Perhaps.'

'No perhaps, Jack. *Definite*. And Leon was doing it through a middleman.'

'Me?' Sefton chortled.

'Medwin thought so.'

'Ah, the late, lamented American. Medwin was way off

base, as they say. He pursued that pet theory of his — that futile suspicion — for years. It got him nowhere.'

'It got him dead.'

'An unfortunate accident, according to my friend Muldowney. Poor "Meddling" Medwin was forever barking up the wrong tree, just as you are right now. Certainly Leon was dabbling in art forgery. No question about it. And that's what you're here for, isn't it?' You're a newspaper man, an investigative journalist, and you're hot on the trail of a scoop. Isn't that it?'

'Something like that.'

'Good, now we're getting somewhere. We're at a point where I may be of immense assistance to you.'

'How?'

'I can tell you how Leon did his forgeries ....'

'I already know that. Can you tell me who killed him?'

'... And even how he disposed of his fakes ....'

'Can you tell me who disposed of him? That's more to the point.'

Sefton shook his head: 'Better leave the murder investigation to the police. I'm discussing what I know of Arthur's forgeries. And I know a great deal.'

'I bet you do.'

'And I'm prepared to give you all that information, all that inside information to add to your scoop, on one condition ....'

'What's that?'

Sefton leaned forward, his tone conciliatory, confidential, chummy: 'We're both men of the world, Joe. You're a journalist, I'm a businessman. I'll give you all you want to know on Arthur's activities on condition that you keep my name, and my family's name, out of it. Look, not only Medwin, but Interpol for Chrissake, tried at one stage to link my name with art forgery. That was some time back. They could prove nothing. Absolutely nothing that could stand up in any court. But I don't want that hoary old chestnut dragged up again. I don't want the publicity. Especially not at this stage. It would embarrass me and it would certainly damage my daughter's future. For my family's sake as much as mine I want our name kept out of all this.'

'Go on.'

'I'm prepared to make you a handsome offer, within reason of course, but a handsome cash settlement nonetheless for the photos and negatives of the painting of my wife that Leon was working on before his death ....'

'His murder.'

'Murder, death — call it what you will! The bastard had it coming to him!' Sefton spoke testily, brushing the interruption aside with an impatient gesture. 'Look Goddard — Joe ... those photos, I want them.'

'Muldowney has them. Police evidence.'

'I know that. Muldowney wouldn't show them to me, but he did tell me what they contained. So I want to make a deal. When they're returned to you, you use all the photos you need for your newspaper piece — all the shots of Leon's body, his forgery studio, everything — *except* any that contain Helen's portrait. Okay? In return I'll give you all the data you need on Leon's forgery techniques, his method of selling them abroad, everything — provided you keep the Sefton name out of it. And in addition I'll throw in a thousand pounds. How about it?'

'The police may not return the photos to me.'

'Okay, two thousand pounds ....'

'I'm not haggling for money Sefton. I'm trying to point out the reality of the situation.' Goddard was also trying to stall, remembering Kelly's injunction to keep Sefton talking as long as possible. 'The police will probably impound those photos, all of them, until after they've completed the murder investigation. For all I know they may hold onto them as court exhibits until after the trial. It could be months before ....'

'Alright. I've considered that.' Sefton leaned over with the brandy decanter, ready to replenish both glasses, but Goddard shook his head. Sefton left down the decanter. 'But when the photos are *eventually* returned to you, as they must be, what's your price for the negatives and the photos of Helen's portrait?'

'Portrait?'

'Portrait, nude study — dammit, I know what it was! Don't play games with me Goddard! How much do you want to keep my wife's picture and my name out of all this?'

But Goddard's stalling game came to an abrupt end with a sharp tap on the door, its sudden opening and the appearance of the manservant.

'Not now Lee! Can't you see I'm busy?'

The servant advanced rapidly, not smiling this time.

'What is it then?' Sefton swung round, the impatience giving way to a kind of urgency. The servant, without once glancing at Goddard, bent forward and whispered something into Sefton's ear.

'The bitch!' With an oath Sefton sprang to his feet. 'What the hell was Karen thinking of!'

He tossed his cigar into the fireplace and turned to Goddard peremptorily: 'Stay here! We'll continue our talk when I get back. Come on Lee!'

Goddard, still lolling back in the armchair, raised his glass in feigned compliance; and Sefton — the mantle of good host already slipping from his shoulders, beginning to unravel, to show dark flaws — hurried from the room with Lee.

They didn't close the door behind them. Goddard stubbed out his cigar in the ashtray, left down his glass, got up, and quickly but noiselessly walked to the door.

The sounds of their running steps came from his left. He peered out and saw the blur of white jacket — Lee chasing dutifully after Sefton — rounding the end of the corridor. Goddard followed. At the end of the corridor he poked his head round the corner, discovered a second carpetted corridor running on for about a dozen yards and at the end of it caught sight of the swinging doors through which they'd just disappeared.

He started forward, eased through the still swinging doors, and found a flight of steps running downwards between narrow, craggy walls. The flight of steps curved to his left. From below somewhere he caught the tang of sea water and heard a splash. The swimming pool? His heart beating wildly, Goddard crept round one short curve and then another, spiralling downwards all the time. He almost stumbled out into the pool area, then quickly pulled himself back. Just a few short steps below his position was a crescent-shaped pool gouged out of the rock, with a tiled patio curving out into the arc of the watery crescent, the whole area roofed in by a broad perspex covering on which the rain continued to drum incessantly. Just before ducking back out of view and flattening himself against the wall he had enough time to glimpse the rocky surrounds of the pool hung with baskets of flowers and trailing plants and to feel the heat wafting up to him. He had the swift impression of a warm, exotic grotto. Something flickered far off in his mind, and was almost lost before he recalled Karen Sefton's words: *the pool is sort of out of bounds today. Daddy says it's something to do with the heating.*

Goddard risked another quick glance. He saw both Karen Sefton and Gloria — the former in a skimpy bikini, the latter in her blue track suit — lying on sunbeds on the patio. Karen was in the act of rising, surprised at the sudden appearance of her father and the manservant.

The two men were hurrying round to the far edge of the pool and peering downwards. They all had their backs to Goddard. He edged out a bit further. And then he saw Kelly ....

She was swimming underwater, gliding along the bottom of the pool, every now and then swinging her legs upwards until they were over her body, her hands exploring the natural rocks and sands on the bottom. As her probing fingers disturbed the sand, sending up little swirling cloudlets in the water, some of the rocks were revealed as — no, not natural rock formations, but carved, rectangular stones of various sizes. The swimmer's hands ran quickly over a short elongated mound, sifting, uncovering a glimpse of a dark, encrusted cylinder, an underwater pipe or — *canon barrel*? Through the shimmering, translucent water Goddard thought he discerned what might even be scroll designs on the submerged stones ....

Suddenly Kelly kicked up towards the surface, her hands straight out in front of her, her long legs rhythmically thrusting her upwards. She broke the surface with a loud sucking for breath, close to the edge of the pool, blinking streaming water from her eyes — and staring into the snub nose of a pistol.

'Okay, Miss Nosy Parker — *out!*'

Sefton was crouched low at the edge, holding the gun only a few feet from Kelly's face. Lost in his admiration of Kelly's lithe body gliding up through the water Goddard hadn't noticed Sefton. Or the gun. Now he moved instinctively towards Sefton, not sure what he was going to do, but suddenly aware that all the emotions of the past few hours — the tangle of fear, suspicion, guesswork, perhaps every emotion since finding Leon's body — was welling up inside him and urging him to action.

He had almost reached Sefton when he heard the cry:

'*Watch out Jack!*'

Sefton came up out of the crouch, bringing the gun round in a wide, vicious swing. The snub-nosed barrel caught Goddard's temple with a jarring force. He went down as if a prop had been knocked out from under him. Through a film of pain and a sudden spread of darkness he crashed down on the tiled patio. Before blacking out his mind was trying to snatch at the dying echo, *Watch out Jack!*

Gloria's voice ....

9

'Wake up ...!'

A toe prodded his shoulder. But it was the intense cold of a stone floor that prised Goddard loose from the void of blackness.

'Come on ... *wake up!*' The voice was far away and unreal, but it succeeded in penetrating the void. The pain in his head returned again with a steady throb.

'Hurry Joe, we've no time!' Kelly's voice.

With a dull flickering his eyes opened, braving the harsh glow from an overhead bulb.

'That's it Joe. Come on!' The naked foot jabbed his shoulder again.

He turned his head. It was a strange sensation to see her wavering form take shape and gradually attain the familiar lines. Kelly was seated just a little distance from him, her feet stretched out and touching his shoulder, her hands behind her back. The strange up-and-down movements of her arms, as if scratching her back, and accompanied by an equally odd rasping sound, had worked the beach-gown down from her shoulders to reveal the still-wet swimsuit clinging to her body. At another time her straining, rhythmic movements might have struck him as erotic.

'Where the hell —?' As he tried to sit up he realised that his hands were tightly bound behind his back. It was the same when he tried to move his feet. Heavy cord was biting into his ankles. 'Where are we?'

'Sefton's boat-house.'

'How long since ...?'

'Since he clobbered you? Ten-fifteen minutes. Are you alright?'

'Are you kidding?' he growled, shaking his head, trying to clear his vision and to work himself into a sitting position. 'What are you doing?'

'Trying to get my hands free.' Kelly had apparently backed herself up against the stern of an old ten-foot open motorboat, half-hidden by plastic covering, and was trying to saw through her bonds by rasping the rope against one of the propeller blades. 'Come on, Joe. Try the other blade. They'll be back soon.'

In a sitting position now, he bumped and jacknifed himself across the cold floor. The slow, jerky movements jolted pain right up to his skull. 'That bastard Sefton ... I'll get him yet!' Goddard's anger was slow, like a burning fuse. A steady, calculating anger.

'That's the spirit. But first we've got to get our hands free ....' Kelly tried to grin through gritted teeth. Beads of perspiration stood out on her forehead. The sawing, rasping sound continued.

'Where are they?'

'Sefton and the Filipino? Somewhere in the house, I think. The women are gone. He sent Mrs Sefton and the daughter back to the hotel.'

Goddard made it to her side. He sat at a right angle to her, trying to locate another propeller blade with his wrists. 'Why the hotel?'

'To search our rooms. Mine in particular. He had the

daughter phone in, pretending to be me. I'm supposed to have given permission for Mrs Sefton to go to my room and fetch some of my things back here for an overnight stay.'

Goddard shook his head, still unable to make sense of it.

'That's why we've got to work fast. When they search through my things they're bound to find my identity. I'm not just an archaeology student, Joe ... I'm *Sergeant* Ashling Kelly, Serious Crimes Squad, Garda Headquarters, Dublin ....'

'Aw Christ ...!' he moaned, starting to scratch his wrists up and down the blunt blade.

'Sorry. I should have told you earlier ....'

'You girls are full of surprises! First Gloria Fontana, now you ....'

'Knew from the start there was something phoney about her ....' Kelly winced, straining against the slowly fraying cords. 'I don't know what her connection with Sefton is, but I don't think she knew anything about the loot at the bottom of the pool.'

'That's another thing. What made you so damned interested in the swimming pool?'

'It had to be the pool if they were looting a submerged wreck.'

'I don't follow.'

'Artefacts, Joe — say from an ancient wreck, Armada maybe — artefacts like that, lying undisturbed on the seabed for hundreds of years, have to remain immersed in sea water to avoid decomposition. You can't suddenly haul them straight up into the light and the fresh air.'

'So, with the sub aqua gear they were hauling them underwater?'

'Canon, culverins, coins, swords, goblets — all in through the submerged gate at the deep end of the pool.

Perfect storage place.'

'And the stones?'

'Ogham stones, dismantled crosses, decorative church doorways ....'

'From the ruined monastery here?'

'Some, but my guess is that most of them came from further afield. And, together with the material from the wreck, what better hiding place than under a layer of sand at the bottom of the family pool? This was the storage depot, the assembly point, before eventual transhipment.'

'How?'

'Ocean-going yacht, fishing boat maybe. God, but this rope is tough ....'

'And this blade is blunt,' he grimaced. He was sweating and his arms were beginning to ache. His wrists were chafing from the taut binding and the pull of the nylon roping. Kelly must be in worse shape, he surmised, if she'd been at this for nearly ten minutes before him. He shot her a sidelong glance. Her eyes were clenched shut and her white teeth biting down hard on her lower lip. Her arms were still moving up and down, but much slower now.

'We're not going to make it Kelly. Not like this ....'

'Shut up and keep sawing ....' she muttered grimly, bravely. 'We've *got* to get free before they come back. We know too much ....'

Goddard redoubled his efforts. He pumped his arms up and down rapidly, sawing, straining, stretching his pained wrists outwards, flexing his forearms so that the rope bit in remorselessly almost to the bone. His face remained grim and expressionless. He was dreadfully aware, and his fear mounted as the seconds passed, that it would have to be he, if anyone, who must extricate Kelly from this situation.

Her shoulders had begun to slump. When he turned and looked down he saw blood oozing from the dark weals encircling her wrists. Only the first of three stands of rope seemed on the verge of parting. Catching his sidelong glance she straightened her shoulders once more and tried to force her arms to work up and down.

'Take it easy Kelly. Leave it to me for a while. You can't keep —'

'*Shush!*' she whispered urgently.

In unison they ceased their work and halted the rasping sounds as a door creaked open somewhere behind them. Footsteps sounded on the stone floor. Goddard tried to look back over his shoulder. He could see nothing, no one. After a brief, tentative pause the footsteps quickened, became bolder, nearer — a woman's steps, almost drowning out the laboured breathing of Kelly and Goddard.

In the next moment Gloria appeared before them, the gleam of a long kitchen knife in her hand. She glanced quickly from Kelly to Goddard and then her gaze faltered. Averting her eyes, she raised the knife.

Before Goddard could divine her intentions she quickly circled behind him, kneeling down. For just a mad, panicky instant he expected to feel the knife plunging in through his shoulder blades or slashing across the front of his throat. Instead he experienced its swift pressure on the rope binding his wrists.

'Sorry the way things worked out Joe,' she mumbled from behind him. She continued in a small voice, the words part contrition, part justification of her point of view. 'Everything I told you about Arty was the honest truth. Only thing I left out was Jack Sefton and me. I met him 'bout a year ago at a cocktail party in London. We've been sorta havin' a thing together since then, you know what I mean ....'

There was a last sudden snap on the rope! Goddard brought his hands round and began to quickly massage his wrists.

'...'Course at that time Jack didn't know I was Arty's Ex. That came later. The thing is, you see, Jack is the guy who's putting up all the cash for this West End show I'm going to be in ....'

Gloria had moved round and was now working on Kelly's bonds. Goddard was starting on the knots securing his feet. 'Go on ....'

'... I guess I panicked a bit back there. Sorry, Joe. I mean, I don't know what other kinda business Jack is mixed up in, but I didn't want you or Goody-Two-Shoes here fucking up my very last chance to break into the big time. Christ I've waited too long for this chance! You've got to believe that Joe. Honest ...!'

'I believe you,' he mumbled, not really caring, snatching at time, frantically working on the knots shackling his ankles.

'I just wanna hit the big time, that's all. I don't want any part in a murder set-up ....'

'Murder?'

'Uh-huh. I heard Jack and the Chink talking about it a few minutes ago. I was kind of listenin' from the kitchen. They plan for the two of you to take a trip out to sea any minute now. The boat — Jack's cabin cruiser, that is — is gonna sink, or blow up or somethin'. Jack's been down there for the past quarter of an hour wirin' it up or puncturin' holes in it or somethin'. It's gonna sink or blow up with you two aboard ....'

'We *three*', Kelly said, exhaling with relief as her bloodied hands were suddenly free.

'Huh?'

'The three of us Gloria. You don't think they're going to let you live to blab about this, do you?' Kelly, like

Goddard, was starting to work on the ankle ropes.

'You mean ...?'

'She means right now the *three* of us are booked in for the voyage. Give me the knife Gloria.' He practically snapped it from her hand. A few deft strokes and his feet were free. He was working quickly on Kelly's bonds when he suddenly became aware of another sound that had been gradually, almost imperceptibly, building up through the steady drumming of the rain — a faint counterpoint in the moist background — the steady purring of an engine. The cabin cruiser?

In the momentary pause to catch at the distant sound, and make sense of it, Goddard's hearing now caught at a different noise. Footsteps. A man's this time ....

He swung round.

'Please carry on, Mr Goddard. We would have had to undo all those knots anyway.' Sefton had loomed up from nowhere, the snub-nosed pistol in his hand and pointing at Goddard's upturned face while still keeping Kelly and Gloria within its narrow, menacing arc. 'Excellent. Now, on your feet. You too, Gloria, my dear.'

In his yellow-orange oilskins Sefton towered triumphantly over them. With his free hand he dragged Gloria to her feet.

'Please, Jack ...!'

'Shut up, you stupid bitch!' He shoved her violently against Goddard. Then, as if relenting somewhat, the beginning of a sardonic smile played on his lips. It failed to reach his eyes as he continued: 'Sorry Gloria, but you dumb blondes will be my ruination yet, I shouldn't wonder. First Karen, now you. Still, there's time yet to drum some sense into my beloved daughter's head, I hope. Now then, all of you, this way please.'

Sefton backed away, walking slowly down the ramp, still keeping the gun trained on them. 'Ready, Lee?'

'Ready sir.' Lee's voice came from somewhere outside. Almost immediately it was followed by the metallic sound of an up-and-over garage-type door being opened. During the scraping sound of the door being pulled up on its chains Kelly had just enough time to draw closer to Goddard and whisper: 'Be ready to jump them on my signal of "but me no buts", okay?'

'Yeah, but ....'

'But me no buts, Joe.'

'Shut up you two!' Sefton snapped. 'Now hurry along please.'

The up-and-over door swung up into its overhead mooring to reveal the sloping ramp running down to a little jetty beside which a thirty-foot cruiser bobbed up and down in the swell. Its engine was humming. Beyond it was the vast rainy panorama of the open sea. In the foreground, sheltering to one side of the open doorway, Lee stood. He was similarly clad in orange oilskins and was carrying a hand gun. Like Sefton's it was aimed at the trio huddled together against the angry stutter of the wind and the squalling rain.

'You'll never get away with this Sefton,' Goddard said, stalling, still trying to buy time.

'I most certainly would have gotten away with it only for the three of you turning up so inexplicably this weekend! Christ, what a series of coincidences, the sort of thing that might never repeat itself in a hundred years — Arthur's stupid murder, Gloria's stupid arrival, your stupid newspaper bungling, this other bitch's stupid busybody-ing around the place! — all in the same week that I'd planned to move all my treasures out of here!'

'How?' Goddard, like Sefton, was shouting above the fury of the storm.

'Never you mind! I offered you a deal — a good deal — but you'd rather throw in your lot with this undercover female cop. So be it ... now *move!*' Sefton stepped behind him, urging him down the ramp. Goddard felt something sharp jab into his back. He knew it had to be the snout of the gun. He braced himself. Sefton pulled back the gun, ready to jab it into Goddard again. But he was expecting the second jab. He glanced swiftly at Kelly to see if she was set. She caught his glance from the corner of her eye ....

'But me no buts —!'

Even as the jabbing snout was leaving his back Goddard was twisting, moving inside and away from the barrel angle, jerking his arm outward with all his might and knocking the gun hand to one side. The automatic exploded deafeningly beside him.

After that all impressions were jumbled, instantaneous, a split-second eruption of separate actions hammering savagely into each other. Goddard only half-heard Gloria's sharp cry, half-glimpsed her body crumpling down on the wet jetty. He'd already spun round, both hands locked about Sefton's forearm, forcing the gun hand away. He half-saw Kelly with her hands reaching up to grab Lee's arm that was about to circle her neck. At the same time she was lashing backwards with her heel. The Filipino went over her shoulder, landed on his back, winded, and slithering along the rain-swept ramp. Goddard and Sefton were still grappling for mastery, Goddard pushing out with all his strength at the gun hand. Sefton's free hand—now a knurled fist—smashed onto Goddard's jaw. He felt his knees buckling, his grip on the gun hand slackening. Still he tried to hold on as Sefton smashed another blow to the side of his neck. Goddard, almost blacking out, fighting for balance on the slippery ground, knew that he was going down ....

Then, just as swiftly, Sefton seemed to be wrenched away from him. Through a haze of pain he saw Sefton doubled up, clutching at the numbing spread of agony in his crotch. As Kelly was lowering her knee she struck out with the edge of her hand to Sefton's wrist, trying to knock the .38 from his grip. The second shot went wild, pinging downwards off the jetty. Kelly got in another blow. Sefton lost balance. He landed on his back, tried to sit up, to focus and bring the automatic to bear. Kelly kicked out again with deadly precision. She caught him on the arm. The gun spun from his hand in a wide loop and splashed into the water.

Lee, the Filipino, was trying to push himself upright; his brown hands were splayed out on the slippery cement of the jetty. The pistol was still clutched in one fist. Goddard stomped down viciously with his heel, twice, crushing the brown fist, loosening the hold on the gun. When it was free — dark, gleaming, lethal metal suddenly smashed out from bloody knuckles — Goddard kicked it to one side and saw it slide over the edge of the jetty and plop into the foamy sea.

Gloria too was sitting in the wet — dazed, disoriented by the pain and the blood welling from a wound in her arm. She was rocking back and forth like an injured child, sobbing and moaning and clutching her damaged elbow. Goddard went to her.

'Fuck off Joe,' she moaned. 'Run for it ....'

Fuck off Gloria, he swore inwardly, taking her good arm and wrenching her to her feet. As she swayed against him Kelly appeared and grabbed Gloria's waist. They started back up the ramp, supporting Gloria between them. With Goddard and Kelly taking her weight on their shoulders Gloria's legs seemed to move of their own volition. They tried to run. The pain in Goddard's jaw surfaced again, jolting him with each rapid step. Despite the pain he jerked his head backwards to find signs of pursuit. He saw Sefton on his knees, shaking his head from side to side, trying to clear his mind of pain and confusion. He saw the Filipino limping towards his lord and master ....

'Move it girls! C'mon!'

They hurried back through the boathouse. Past the ten-foot motor boat with its plastic covering and blunt propeller blades and pieces of frayed rope. Past their earlier agony. They quickly found the still open doorway. The path, Y-shaped, led two ways — left, under another perspex awning, just a few paces to the kitchen side of the house — and the other way, right, through rain-swaying shrubbery, along a garden path that seemed to sweep round to the front of the house.

'Which way?' Kelly begged.

'To the right,' Goddard commanded, hitching Gloria further up on his shoulder.

They hurried on, sloshing into dark puddles, bustling through showery sprays of fronds and little branches and tangly plants.

'I can't go on ....' Gloria sobbed.

'Come on Gloria, we can do it!' Kelly, with a kind of superhuman effort, almost lifted the other woman up and dragged her round to the front of the house ....

And there, right before them — only a few yards away! — stood the station wagon. The headlights were still on, the driver's door wide open ....

Helen Sefton and Karen were at the top of the steps, standing like statues by the front door, transfixed, as though stunned by the so-recent gunfire — or by the sudden emergence from the rainy shadows of this bedraggled trio? Helen Sefton ran back down the steps when she saw that they were making for the car. Kelly quickly detached herself from the burden of Gloria, leaving her to Goddard, and ran to meet Mrs Sefton. As Goddard dragged Gloria to the car, wrenching open the back door and bundling her in, he was aware of Kelly confronting Mrs Sefton. When he saw Kelly feinting expertly, side-stepping and then knocking the older woman to the ground with some kind of Judo throw, he jumped into the driving seat.

The keys were still in the ignition. He flung open the other door for Kelly as he tugged at the choke. The engine fired at the first attempt. Kelly tumbled in beside him just as Sefton and Lee came racing round the side of the house. Goddard saw that Sefton had dug up another gun from somewhere ... seeing them tumbling into the car Sefton halted suddenly, feet planted apart, his arms jerking upwards as he tried to take aim with a long-barrelled rifle, or shotgun? Goddard didn't have time to identify the weapon. There was a wet, squelching scream of tyres as the car bucked out and veered crazily. The passenger door was still swinging wildly as Goddard dragged the steering wheel over. One shot, silent because of the engine's roar, shattered the glass of the swinging door. Kelly crouched down and clung to Goddard as he slewed the car towards Sefton's shadowy figure. Sefton dived out of its path and Goddard rapidly changed direction, crashing through the wooden fence and out into the night. Splinters of wood showered the bonnet from the impact and another shot splattered the rear window. Then the car was heaving over a short stretch of moorland, bouncing and jumping perilously until Goddard found the lane. The headlights blazed through the sheets of rain.

He turned in his seat, and, risking a backward glance, saw nothing in the direction of the Laurels. Feeling free — at least for the moment — Goddard was almost elated.

'Where to, Kelly?'

She was reaching out and trying to haul in the passenger door. The collision with the fence had buckled it so that it wouldn't close properly. She had to grip the door handle and hold it firmly as it rattled and shook with each bounce of the car.

'Where to? Muldowney's?'

She shook her head: 'To Jack Sweeney's. I'll explain when we get there. Slow down a bit Joe. I better take a look at Gloria.'

'Oh yeah,' he muttered, dropping down to thirty. 'How are you doing back there?'

Gloria's only response was a whimpered oath. Kelly gave up her tussle with the door, letting it swing freely and scrape and tear and batter against the low bushes and stone walls of the laneway. When she was clambering over the seat and into the back Goddard rolled down his window. He stuck his head into the rushing gulf of air, listening for the sounds of pursuit. There was only an eerie silence lying beyond the wind and the pelting rain and the clattering roar of their escape.

'Any sign of Sefton's Toyota?'

Kelly didn't answer. He rolled the window back up. His eyes, straining to pick out the dark grey murkiness of the lane, now shifted to the overhead mirror. Kelly had pulled the belt from her sodden beach gown and was fashioning it into a tourniquet around Gloria's bicep. When she'd finished she started to use the hem of the gown to wipe away the bloody streaks below the elbow.

'That bad, huh?'

'No, it's only a flesh wound I think. Still, best to be on the safe side.'

'You're sure I'm not bleeding to death?' Gloria asked.

'No way, Gloria.'

'Jesus, it could've been my leg. That would've really fucked up my dancing career!'

From where he was sitting it struck Goddard that Gloria sounded healthy enough. Still, he booted up to forty-forty-five with his hands gripping the wheel and sweating as he drove on through the rainy twilight.

When they were skirting the top of the harbour road he heard the chatter of a helicopter away out over the sea, in the direction of the mainland. He turned round, shooting a questioning glance at Kelly.

'Detectives. Murder Squad. Good old Sean Muldowney — he must have gotten through!'

'Murder squad? So, it's show-down time,' he grimaced.

'Don't worry, Joe,' Kelly said, leaning over and placing her hand on his shoulder. 'You were terrific back there, do you know that?'

'You weren't too bad yourself,' he grinned, removing one hand from the wheel and closing it over hers.

When he pulled the car to a slewing halt outside Sweeney's isolated cottage he looked back behind him and saw the landing lights of the helicopter flickering down somewhere near the hotel.

Show down time ....

10

To his surprise Goddard found Muldowney waiting at the doorway of Sweeney's cottage. His appearance didn't seem to surprise Kelly, though.

'In God's name! What's happened at all?' The policeman hurried towards them, glancing rapidly at each in turn, taking in the bloodstains on the hem of Kelly's beach-gown, the tourniquet on Gloria's arm and their combined sodden, dishevelled appearance. 'Holy Mother of the Divine Saviour!'

'Relax Sean,' Kelly said. 'It's not nearly as bad as it looks.'

'No?' Gloria shrieked. 'I was nearly *murdered* — we were *all* nearly murdered by that bastard Sefton and the little Chink!'

'Let's first take a look at that wound, Miss Fontana, and then get ye all into some dry clothes and then you can tell me all about it.' Muldowney ushered them into the remembered room with its sports trophies on the sideboard, its glass case with the huge, stuffed fish on the chimneybreast, the fishing rods suspended on their brass hooks, and the mantelpiece full of pipe-racks and tobacco tins. A full, blazing peat fire reached out to them with its welcoming blast of heat. There was no sign of Sweeney.

Muldowney indicated one of a pair of matching doors leading off the lounge and they took Gloria through to a neat little bedroom. Kelly put her sitting on the edge of the bed and undid the tourniquet and carefully rolled up the sleeve for Muldowney's inspection. 'It was dark in the car, and bouncing all over the place ....'

'Thanks a lot,' Goddard muttered, suddenly tired. He sat down on a pouffe and searched for his cigarettes.

'... And I couldn't see too well. I thought it best to ....'

'You did right, Ashling. Now, let's take a look.' Muldowney carefully examined the wound and then asked Gloria to move her arm. She did so, gingerly, silently, without a whimper. 'Good. It's no more than a fleabite Miss. Now, like a good girl, Ashling, could I ask you to fetch a First Aid box that Jack keeps somewhere out in the kitchen ....'

Goddard, lighting a cigarette, let his eyes wander aimlessly about the room. He was suddenly struck by its odd variance—its vivid contrast—to the masculine character of the lounge outside. This was clearly a woman's room. A young woman's at that ....

It had all the delicate and pretty feminine touches of decoration, chintzy little curtains with bows, lacy fol-de-rols, a shelf full of old teddy bears and put-away dolls, pop music posters festooning two walls and almost obliterating the pink flowers of the wallpaper, a stereo unit in the midst of an untidy spill of albums and cassettes on the floor in one corner.

Muldowney, following his gaze, read his thoughts: 'Nelly Sweeney's room. Jack's daughter. She went over to the mainland yesterday. Ah, good girl, Ashling.'

She'd returned with a plastic box emblazoned with a little red cross.

'You people best be gettin' into somethin' dry. Soon as

I've dressed this wound for you Miss, Ashling here will help you pick out a few dry things from Nelly's wardrobe. As to yourself, Mr Goddard, if you wouldn't mind goin' into the next room you'll no doubt find some ould sweater and trousers belongin' to Jack ....'

'*I* don't mind. Will *he*?'

'Jack Sweeney is island born and reared. We've a sayin' hereabouts that there's nothin' so small that it can't be shared. Sure Jack'd give you the shirt off his own back.'

'A sweater and slacks will do nicely, thanks.'

It was when he was rising wearily from the pouffe that Goddard saw Nelly Sweeney — or, rather, her likeness. On the little bedside table stood a mounted, studio-type photograph of a pretty teenager, fair-haired, freckled, smiling shyly. Hanging from a little chain about her neck, and nestling innocently between the slight adolescent protuberance of young breasts that scarcely riffled the front of her white blouse, was a Claddagh ornament — two hands holding a heart and surmounted by a crown. The symbols of Love, Fidelity and Honour. Instantly he recalled the charred sketch-book. He turned quickly to Kelly. She followed his gaze and his meaning. Then, with a brief, almost imperceptible nod that seemed to signify the advisability of silence, she moved over to the wardrobe, removing her wet beachgown.

'Okay, Gloria, let's see what fits ....'

'To hell with the fit! Let's see what's warm and dry.'

'You too, Mr Goddard. Better get out of those things before you catch your death of cold ....'

'Yeah, it would never do to cheat the hangman, would it?'

Muldowney followed him out, closing the door on the ladies.

'Don't you want to hear what happened at Sefton's?'

'All in good time, Mr Goddard. All in good time. I'm sure Ashling will explain everythin' when ....'

'I see. One cop to another.'

'She told you, then?'

'No one tells me anything! I'm not sure what the hell is going on anymore – walking into some kind of trap at the Laurels, helicopters flying in, you waiting for us here as though you'd planned it with Kelly, Sweeney's absence, his daughter's photo in there with that necklace thing that Leon had sketched! — I just don't know what the fuck is happening!'

'All in good time. Now get changed like a good man. Please.'

Ten minutes later they were all re-assembled by the fireside – Gloria, Kelly and Goddard in an assortment of ill-fitting sweaters, slacks, slippers and shoes, Muldowney alone looking normal in his uniform and with a tray-load of steaming mugs of Bovril ready for them.

'Got nothing stronger?' Gloria scowled at her mug. 'I'm an invalid, remember?'

Muldowney shook his head: 'Jack keeps nothin' stronger on the premises, I'm afraid. Even if he did I'd draw the line at requisitionin' a man's liquor.' He turned to Ashling: 'Well then, Sergeant, I'll let you take over —'

'*Sergeant?*' Gloria looked from one face to the next. 'What the hell is this sergeant bit? Would someone mind explaining to me what —'

Ashling never did get her chance to explain ....

At that moment the front door burst open. Sefton was standing there with a double barrelled shot-gun aimed right at them. Rain gleamed viciously on the long barrels menacing them.

'Don't move! Stay right where you are!' Sefton edged

in. He was still wearing the yellow oilskins and his sea boots were covered in dark, peaty mud. He closed the door behind him, cutting out the snarling wind and the gusts of rain.

'Do as he says,' Kelly commanded in a low, even voice.

'That's more like it.' Suppressed anger still showed through Sefton's taut features.

'If you're thinking of using that gun then let me warn you ....'

'Shut up, you meddling bitch!'

'... That you'll never get away with it. Not *four* of us.'

'Shut up or you'll be first to get it!'

Muldowney tried to take over, to deflect the growing anger: 'Listen, Mr Sefton, at this very moment there's a helicopter-load of detectives on the island. Surely you must realise that you haven't a chance of ....'

'Haven't I?' Sefton still kept the barrels trained on the tight-knit group. 'Ever heard of hostages? That's right, *hostages*! Three of you should be sufficient for my purposes.'

'And the fourth?' Goddard waited, the tension seeping back into him, as Sefton continued.

'The fourth — that's you, Goddard — will have to be content with a mere knee-capping job. When the chopper-load of cops find you here you can relay my message. It's quite simple ... hands off, or I'll dispose of the other hostages one by one. I *mean* it! I've spent too long on this project, years of planning ....'

'Looting,' Kelly snapped.

'... And only for this infernal storm, and then the four of you snooping and butting in, I would've had all my stuff out of the Laurels by tomorrow! I'm that close to bringing it off. There's a French yacht only forty miles from here waiting ....' He suddenly broke off. 'Right, on your feet! You too, Goddard. You'll get yours outside. I don't want any funny business behind my back.'

'Please Jack,' Gloria begged, an edge of hysterics in her voice. 'We've done nothing to ....'

'*Move it!*'

'You're wasting your time Gloria,' Ashling took Gloria by the hand. 'He's mad!'

'He's also wasting his time,' Goddard added with a kind of reckless defiance, trying desperately to play for time, for some tiny advantage somehow, somewhere. 'Only a complete nut-case would fail to see that he hasn't a snowball's chance in hell of abducting you three people and —'

'Shut fucking up!' Sefton snarled as he jerked open the door. 'We'll soon see who's the nut-case in a moment when his knees are cut from under him! Now then, you first Muldowney. Then the ladies. You last, Goddard. You're expendable.' He laughed viciously — and Goddard suddenly realised that he'd been right; the guy *was* mad. 'Now listen carefully. You walk slowly, in single file, and straight towards the car. In case any of you get any funny ideas just remember that you'll be in my line of vision all the time. At close quarters this weapon can make mincemeat of the lot of you. Now move!'

Sefton stood well back from them, wary, circling behind them and out of range of any sudden lunge. Goddard saw the cocked hammers and the finger on the first trigger.

'That's it, nice and easy. One at a time ....'

Muldowney led off, stepping out into the whorls of rain trapped in the still-blazing headlights of the station wagon. The elderly policeman glanced to neither left nor right. Neither did the girls. They walked steadily out into the night towards the car. The metal snouts of the gun jabbed sharply into the small of Goddard's back. He half-turned from the sudden force of the blow as he was going out through the doorway ....

And there he saw Jack Sweeney just to his right, the iron-grey hair plastered down on his forehead by the streaming rain, the immense bulk of the man flattened back against the ivy-covered wall as he hid from view. Sweeney had just time to signal with a sudden jerk of his head, urging Goddard to follow the others towards the car. Goddard, quickened his pace, still half-turned, glimpsing the long barrels preceding Sefton out the door.

Then he flung himself to one side as the twin barrels were suddenly jerked upwards and high by the sweeping power and grip of Sweeney's hands. The first shot tore up into the night. Goddard spun round. Sweeney and Sefton were wrestling in the doorway, silhouetted against the light from within. As Goddard rushed back to the door — Kelly and Muldowney a foot or two behind him and flanking him — he heard the deafening report of the second shot. For just an instant the men in the doorway swayed in a kind of drunken dance. Then, with a last — almost superhuman – effort Sweeney wrenched the gun from his adversary, drew backwards and up, and then smashed the butt down on Sefton's jaw. There was a horrible sound of hard wood crashing into bone and then both men slithered to the ground. Sefton, senseless, his jaw smashed and bloody, fell backwards into the room. Sweeney sprawled and moaned softly against the doorpost.

Goddard tried to hold Kelly back, to shield her from the awful sight of so much blood. But she pushed past him. Muldowney had already reached the doorway. When Goddard came up to him Muldowney was bending over Sweeney.

'How is he?'

Sweeney's lolling head was cradled in the policeman's arms, the sleeves of the uniform drenched with blood and rain. They tried to prop the dying man against the wall but he kept sinking further into the mire. Muldowney was quietly intoning the words of the Act of Contrition into Sweeney's ear. Sweeney's eyes were closed, his breathing low and harsh. His features — the great granite jaw, the flattened nose, the scarred cheek — were twisted and flexed with pain, but he kept nodding his comprehension, kept trying to mumble the prayer in unison with his neighbour.

'... Who, for Thy infinite goodness, art so deserving of all my love and I firmly resolve, by Thy holy grace, never more to offend Thee ....'

Death, and the last words of the prayer, came together. The policeman gently released the lolling head and stood up. He shook his head from side to side — sad, bemused, confounded by the futility of it all — and then, as if speaking to himself, or echoing something of the recent prayer, he mumbled: 'Maybe 'tis better this way. 'Twouldn't have sat easy with me to be chargin' poor Jack Sweeney with the murder of Arthur Leon ....'

He walked past Goddard without another word or glance. With all the rain it was hard to tell if there were tears on Muldowney's cheeks.

11

'What made you suspect Sweeney?' Goddard asked, finger-plopping some ice into his glass and then passing the half-empty whiskey bottle over to Muldowney.

'There was a number of things to it. No one of them for certain, but all together addin' up.'

'Such as?'

Goddard started an involuntary yawn, then remembered his sore jaw from Sefton's punch. It seemed such a long time ago. To fight off the yawn, and to stretch his legs, he got off the bed and moved over to the window and pulled back the curtains with one hand, swirling the ice-and-whiskey glass in the other. Pale light, the stealthy vanguard of dawn, was touching the sea and the shadowy outlines of the mainland. The rain had stopped a few hours ago. The sea looked calm and smooth, and he thought he heard the faint, steady *chug-chug* of the ferry, but he couldn't be sure. There was too much noise from downstairs.

They were in Goddard's hotel room, behind closed doors, happy to have at last escaped the detective officers, the scores of reporters from the Dublin and British papers, the wire service men, the mobile TV crews from the networks, the officials from the National Museum, all still milling about below in the bar and the lobby. Reporters were still arriving by ferry, according to a very tired, happy Murty (who'd already sold four of his sea-daubs in return for 'inside' information) and an ecstatic Mammy who'd already sold out all her rooms for four times their off-season price, and who'd had to hastily recall all the local holiday staff with a promise of time-and-a-half in order to cope. Business was booming.

For Goddard too. After the police interviews — mercifully brief, thanks to the good offices and recommendations of Kelly and Muldowney — he'd gotten his story off first. Well before any of the others had arrived. A worldwide exclusive, with pictures, his London editor now winging it all around Europe and the States, tying up all sorts of syndication deals. He was happy. He was tired. He was too exhilarated to sleep. And most of all he was curious ....

'You haven't answered my question.'

'What? Oh ....' Muldowney roused himself. He'd been on the point of dozing off in the armchair.

'I wanted to know what made you first suspect Sweeney?'

'A number of things. Did I ever tell you, Mr Goddard ....'

'Call me Joe.'

'Fair enough, Mr Goddard. And if it pleases you, I suppose you might call me Sean, as I'm off duty now, like ....'

'You were saying, Sean?'

'Yes, did I ever tell you Joe that it's been my experience that solutions to the deepest mysteries lie in the hearts and minds of people — did I ever tell you that?' Muldowney's hand wavered above the whiskey bottle.

'Yes, I seem to remember you saying something like that. Go on.' Goddard moved away from the window.

'Hearts and minds. And local gossip.' Muldowney began to trickle some more whiskey into his glass. "Course, in my line o' business it doesn't do to listen to *all* the local gossip and ould wives tales. Still, from time to time you come across the odd *smidgeen* of information. Not, mind you, that you'd want to pay too much heed to every whisper about which poor young one is in the family way, or which of them is makin' the trip to Dublin, and then to an English abortion clinic. Or to listen to ould wans sayin' that such carry on is neither Irish, Catholic or patriotic, and why don't the girls stay at home and give all that work to Irish doctors ....'

'Will you get to the point Sean.' Goddard sat down again opposite him.

'The point, yes. Well, the point is Joe, that I heard one or two of them rumours about young Nelly, and that lately she'd been goin' down to Owls Watch to have her portrait done. And the rumours had it that the blackguard Leon did more than her portrait, worse luck. And no doubt poor Jack heard the same rumours. Whether or which, it was as plain as a pikestaff that when he was leavin' her over to the mainland on the ferry yesterday, Nelly had put on a bit of weight. It's my theory that on the trip over Jack questioned her, learnt the truth of things and the name of the culprit.'

'Hardly a motive for murder?'

'To a man like Jack Sweeney it might be — for most of the older folk hereabouts that sort of disgrace, 'specially at the hands of a worthless pup of an outsider such as Mr Arthur Leon who'd never have the decency to wed with the lass he'd injured! — with them, and with Jack Sweeney, 'twould easily be a cause for instant retribution.'

'And that's *all* — you based all your suspicion on *that*?'

'Ah no,' Muldowney said. 'No, as I said, there was a number of things to it. D'you remember when I first met you at Sweeney's cottage yesterday, after you and Miss Fontan' called there to report the findin' of Mr Leon's dead body?'

'Yeah, sure.'

'Well Joe, I wouldn't have expected you to notice anythin' out of place there, seein' as how 'twas your first visit to Jack Sweeney's ....'

'Out of place — what?'

'The shot-gun. Jack's shot-gun. Did you notice that there were only his fishin' rods above the mantelpiece?'

'Yes.'

'Normally the shot-gun should've been hangin' up among the rods. I knew the place. I noticed it was missin'. Gave me food for thought, in view of the fact that yourself and Miss Fontan' said that Leon had been killed by the blast of a shot-gun. 'Course, it didn't necessarily prove anything ....'

'What *did* then?'

'Nothin' in particular. But the other thing was when we were lookin' over your photographs in my office — you, me and Miss Fontan' — and the three of us discussin' how a murder victim often tries to leave some indication as to the identity of the attacker, a sign of some sort.'

'I think that was your idea Sean.'

'Was it? Ah well then, sure I might not have been too far off the mark.'

'I don't follow.'

'The mark, Joe. The slash of paint on the cheek. When Miss Fontan' came up with the idea that her late husband was holding the paint brush in his left hand — indicatin' maybe that the killer was left-handed — she may have been close to the truth. That got me thinkin'. And examinin' your photos. Perhaps it wasn't the left-hand, but the slash of paint on the cheek ....'

'A scar — Jack Sweeney had a pronounced scar on his

left cheek!'

'Exactly. That, plus the missin' shot-gun from the chimney breast, plus the rumours about young Nelly's condition, plus my own instinct of how someone like poor Jack would react to such knowledge, plus my experience that ....'

'The deepest mysteries lie, not so much in physical clues, but in the hearts and minds of people ....' Goddard finished it for him, nodding slowly, comprehendingly.

'After that I just had to notify poor Jack that I'd be droppin' in to see him and to discuss Arthur Leon's murder. Not a pleasant task, Joe, but I knew that I wouldn't have to come armed and I knew that Jack wouldn't try to bluff or lie or threaten. He did what he felt he had to do, and he knew that I'd have to do my duty. We're simple enough people hereabouts ....' Muldowney took a sip from his glass, dolefully, not really relishing it.

'And Kelly knew about all this, knew you'd be there at Sweeney's cottage?'

Muldowney nodded: 'Ashling was conductin' her own investigation. You know, the plunder of our national heritage. I was conductin' me first-ever investigation into a murder crime. But we were working closely together on both matters.'

'I see. So she arranged to come with us to the Laurels and snoop around and then join you later at Sweeney's place?'

'Yes. Y'see Joe, me niece had to —'

'Your niece — *Kelly?*'

'Didn't she tell you? Ah yes, Ashling is me sister Eileen's daughter. Eileen's husband — that's me brother-in-law Mick — is a Chief Superintendent above in Dublin. When Ashling finished her archaeology studies and couldn't find a suitable academic position her daddy encouraged her to join the Force ....'

'You're worse than the Mafia!' Goddard shook his head from side to side.

'Bedad we're not. We're a law-abiding family, so we are!' Muldowney said with evident pride as he reached for his glass.

There was a knock at the door. 'It's me, Ashling ....'

Goddard hurried over and unbolted it. Kelly — in jeans and a tight-fitting black sweater — entered, balancing a tray containing a teapot, three cups and a plate of sandwiches. 'Only cheese,' she smiled. 'Murty's run out of ham.'

'Cheese is fine, girl,' Muldowney began to clear a place on the tiny coffee table for the laden tray. 'So?'

'So everything is okay Uncle Sean.' She put down the tray and began to pour tea into the cups. 'We've already located the French yacht and impounded it. It's the *one* alright. Specially constructed sea-water tanks to transport the booty from the bottom of Sefton's pool, a concealed hold for the other artefacts ....'

'What about the Seftons?' Muldowney was already munching into one of the sandwiches.

'All in custody. All formally charged. He's been flown to the mainland. Hospitalised under tight guard. The ladies charged as accessories. Also the inscrutable little Oriental gent ....'

'And Gloria?'

'What about her?' Kelly gazed at Goddard over the brim of her cup.

'For God's sake Kelly — okay, *sergeant* Kelly! — what about Gloria?'

'Well, as you are aware,' she paused, sipped, teased, 'Miss Fontana's wound was only a slight one and therefore ....'

'I'm not talking about the damn scratch! What about *her* — her connection with Sefton?'

'Oh *that*? Miss Fontana's amorous involvement with Sefton, or any other man, is no concern of mine. All my report contained was that she was instrumental in assisting us to escape, that without her we were finished.'

Goddard's taut expression relaxed. He flashed her a brief appreciative smile: 'Thanks Kelly.'

'As a matter of fact I think Miss Fontana has finally made the big time, show-biz wise, as they say.'

'What do you mean?'

'Well, it seems that my report has made her the heroine of the entire escapade. At this very moment she's down in the bar, surrounded by a dozen TV chaps and newspaper reporters, all begging to sign her up for chat show programmes and newspaper serialisations and smiling charmingly into flash-bulbs and cameras and enjoying herself immensely. At any rate she's the star of the show and I understand that her London agent is already on his way here with a sheaf of contracts.'

'Isn't it the truth,' Muldowney muttered, wiping breadcrumbs from his mouth, 'the greatest war that ever was someone always comes safe out of it like a hero.'

'Thanks Kelly,' Goddard repeated.

She laid down her cup and saucer and came over, seating herself beside him on the edge of the bed. 'Don't mention it Joe. Anything for a friend.'

'What about you and Sean here? Medals and promotions I suppose?'

She grinned, shaking her head from side to side. 'All in the line of duty. We've still got an awful lot of paperwork ahead of us tomorrow.'

'And then?'

Her shoulders hunched up in a delicate little shrug.

Goddard took her hand. 'I'm due to head back to Dublin tomorrow. I could always hang around for a day or two, if you like ….'

'I won't have much free time Joe.'

He was gazing into the dark, luminous eyes. 'I know that Kelly, but ....'

She silenced him with a quick smile, and the tip of her forefinger sketching a rapid, delicate command on his lips. She whispered, 'But me no buts Joe ....'

Then suddenly her face drew closer and the restraining fingertip was replaced by her lips. It was a long, slow, lingering kiss ....

Muldowney tip-toed to the door. As he opened it he looked back and grinned: 'Yerra, wouldn't you think now that a university-educated lass and a newspaper gent would know the old saying that "the first sigh of love is the last sigh of wisdom" ....'

But Goddard and Kelly didn't hear him. Not even after he closed the door and went whistling merrily down the corridor ....

GLENDALE CRIME SERIES

PUBLISH OR PERISH? H.J. Forrest

A Dublin University, plagued by death and staff rivalries, calls in the Murder Squad ....

———

CALL ME EVIL Desmond Moore

Dublin writer, Alan Firth, is lured to Scotland and then to France to settle a dead man's account ....

———

COGAN'S CASE Howard R. Simpson

A murdered Frenchman and an international drug trafficking ring. But this wasn't Miami, this was West Cork ....

———

MURDER PAINTS A PORTRAIT Vincent Caprani

On a storm-lashed island off the west coast of Ireland, Joe Goddard hit upon the biggest art heist of the decade ....

———

ROGAN Desmond Moore

Who was Rogan? Rogan was a chessboard piece long overdue for removal ....

———

SNUFF Myles Dungan & Jim Lusby

No one wanted to publicise the fact that there was a serial killer on the loose in RTE's Montrose studios ....